FEUD AT BROKEN SPOKE

FEUD AT BROKEN SPOKE

•

TERRELL L. BOWERS

The characters and events portrayed in this book are fictitious. Any similarity to real persons, living or dead, is coincidental and not intended by the author.

Printed in the United States of America.

Published by AmazonEncore
P.O. Box 400818
Las Vegas, NV 89140

ISBN-13: 9781477836231
ISBN-10: 1477836233

For my wonderful daughters, Melanie and Nicole

This title was previously published by Avalon Books; this version has been reproduced from the Avalon book archive files.

Chapter One

Timony Fairbourn stopped her horse atop the rise for a breather. She straightened her legs, applying pressure to the stirrups, and rose up in the saddle. Then, leaning back against the cantle, she arched her back to relieve the stiffness. She was glad that spring roundup was the only time she was expected to help out on the range. Rolling out of bed an hour before sunup, on the back of a horse sixteen hours, then riding patrol at nights to keep the separated steers from wandering back to the main herd, it was not her idea of a good time.

John Fairbourn, the eldest of the family, was a mile or two away, working with Token Haines and the others, branding calves. Timony experienced a sense of pride, thinking of her brother. He was the backbone of the family and it was he who had made Rocking Chair Ranch one of the best in the country. Eight years older than Billy, her other brother, and ten years her senior, he was more like a father than a brother.

Relaxing her posture, she visually swept the horizon for any stray cattle while her consciousness took a melancholy journey down memory lane. John had assumed the role of family monarch, upon the death of their father. His strength and maturity had lessened the impact of the loss to the family. Timony perceived a trace of guilt at the thought. It seemed to her callous and insensitive that she had not mourned his passing to a greater extent.

Contrarily, her mother's death, which had occurred when she was only five years old, still haunted her endlessly. It could have been the fact that she grew up in a house full of men, or that Timony was forced to become the woman of the house before her teens, but she believed it was something more fundamental. Perhaps it was the need of every child to have a mother, to feel secure in her arms, to feel loved, and be tucked in at night. She viewed mothers as maternal angels, whose job it was to oversee their children from infants to juveniles, to early teenage years, and finally to adulthood. She reasoned that John had been there to fulfill the father figure in her life, so it followed that she missed her mother all the more.

Not that Timony had been completely without a woman in her life. Linda Haines, the wife of their foreman, did much of the cooking and helped with the laundry and such, but they had a separate house and private lives. While Linda had taught Timony to cook and do chores around the house, she was not an outgoing or openly compassionate woman. In no way did having her close by compensate for the loss of her mother.

For a time, Timony stared sightlessly across the expansive fields, attempting to picture her mother in her mind's eye. It had been so long, fifteen lonely years. The image was there, but it was distorted, the features undefined.

How tragic, she thought, *I can't even form a clear picture of my own mother. I've forgotten what she looked like!*

The sound of a horse's hooves pounding the earth broke her pensive reflection. She twisted in the saddle enough to see Billy approaching. As was his habit, he rode his horse hard. John had gotten after him a number of times, but Billy never changed. He enjoyed working his mount, but was careful never to go beyond the point of exhaustion.

Timony often envied her brother's devil-may-care attitude, the way he took just about anything in stride. The loss of their mother had to have been difficult for him too, but he had seldom mentioned it. Billy was not the sentimental type, not on the surface, at least. Timony loved him dearly, but she sometimes grew impatient with the way he viewed life as an endless array of jokes and good times.

"Hey, Sis!" Billy said, pulling his mount to a halt, displaying his ready simper. "Sure am glad it's you up here. Thought for a moment that someone had gone and put a scare-thief on the hill."

"A what?"

"You know how the farmers sometimes use a scarecrow out in their fields to keep the crows away from their corn?"

"Yes, I know what a scarecrow is."

"Well, I figured someone had stuck a scare-thief up here"—his grin widened—"to keep the rustlers away."

Timony gave her head a shake. "Up before daylight, pounding leather for endless hours, I don't know how you can have the energy for making dumb jokes."

"Dumb?" He blinked. "Maybe lame, silly, or even in poor taste sometimes, but dumb?"

"I thought you were working the south end," she said to change the subject.

"Was, until I cut the trail of some stragglers, six or eight head, I'd say."

Timony was assailed by an immediate anguish. "Don't tell me—moving toward the Cline place?"

"Like geese heading south."

Timony reined her horse that direction. "Darn their worthless hides! After all of our trouble to keep an eye on them. Dexter will be out for blood!"

"It ain't our fault," Billy replied. "We've been running ourselves ragged trying to keep the cattle away from his crops."

Timony didn't argue the point. Dexter Cline had set up an unholy fuss the last time a few head of cattle got into his crops. He was going to be blistering mad if it happened again.

She couldn't blame him for being angry. A number of times, she had ridden past and seen him and his four kids slaving away in the fields. They were honest, hard-working people, trying to scratch out a meager existence in a very hard and unforgiving land. The cattle were an added challenge that the Cline family didn't need.

Using her riding spurs, she urged her horse into a run. Billy was at full gallop at her side. It was five or six miles to the Cline ranch. With the cattle having a huge start, she feared they had little chance to head them off.

It was catch-up day for the Cline household. Outside the house, Dexter and the only boy in the family, Jimmy, were busy at work. Jimmy was sitting in the shade, exchanging the worn husks on the broom with the shave stalks they had stored from the last year's broomcorn crop. Dexter was a short distance away, using a rasp to file an edge on the field hoes.

Within the house, Sally and June took turns working the handle on the centrifugal churn, making butter. Across the room, Leta was on her knees, helping her mother clean the huge, ornate, cast-iron stove that served for heating and cooking. The oven, firebox, and clean-out all had to be scrubbed or emptied regularly; as well, the water reservoir had to be constantly filled, and wood or cow chips stockpiled for fuel.

Leta paused from scrubbing to rest. "When I get married," she complained, sitting back on her heels, "I'm going to get a potbellied stove for heat and do my cooking over the hearth. A fireplace has got to be less of a chore than cleaning this iron monster every month."

"And where are you going to get the wood, Leta?" her mother, Helen Cline, asked. "You need a bed of hot coals to cook pies, bake loaves of soda bread, or roast or simmer your dinners. In case you hadn't noticed, there isn't any fruitwood about, no hardwood at all, in fact. Sagebrush and cow chips don't offer sufficient coals for maintaining a constant heat. Without that, you can't bake a good many things. Are you going to live on boiled foods from the pot?"

"That might beat standing over this stove for hours, constantly feeding it fuel and wilting from the heat. I swear, it's hotter cooking up a big meal than it is hoeing out in the fields under the summer sun."

"I agree with Leta," June offered, relaxing from her turn of working the handle on the butter churn. "I want a small cooking stove and a fireplace. Maybe another stove for heating the house and warming the water, but that's it."

"You don't want a house," her mother quipped, "you want a warehouse of different stoves."

"Couldn't use up more space than ours. It takes up the whole kitchen."

"And it weighs a ton," Sally put in. "If you own one like ours, you have to put the stove where you want it first and then build the house around it."

"We're lucky to have such a luxury," Helen told the girls seriously. "It's one of the few in all of Broken Spoke."

"Maybe there's a message in that," Leta joked.

"I don't think—" Helen began, but was interrupted by Jimmy rushing to the door of the house.

"Come a-running!" he shouted. "We've got cattle at the upper end of the cornfield!"

Everyone stopped what they were doing, scrambled to their feet and raced for the door. Dexter was rushing toward them, as they filed outside.

"You girls get up there!" he shouted. "Jimmy! grab up Pokey!"

Leta led Sally and June, all three running toward the cornfield as fast as they could. Jimmy scampered over to the plow horse, swung up onto its back, and started it moving. He attempted to get the worn-out plug to break into a run. Instead, the ungainly trot of the big horse caused him to bounce about on its back like a jackrabbit with the hiccups.

At the most distant end of the cornfield, the cattle milled about, happily gorging themselves. With a wrap of their tongue and a twist of their necks, they pulled up tender stalks of corn by the roots. The three girls arrived, waving their arms and screaming at the tops of their voices, trying to drive the cattle back. The animals begrudgingly rambled away from the noisy trio, but trampled more of the crop under their hooves.

Dexter grabbed his rifle from the house. He hurried off toward the commotion, irate enough to start pumping lead at the destructive cattle. Before he was able to get close enough to do any shooting, two riders appeared in the distance. With a determined stride, he began the long walk out to the far end of the field.

Billy rode in among the cattle, whistled loudly, and used the end of his lariat to pop the cattle on the hindquarters. A few swats, a yell or two, and he had them on the run. Once the animals were clear of the field, he hazed them back toward the rolling hills and the Rocking Chair range.

Timony Fairbourn stopped her horse and waited for Dexter to arrive. She read the frustration and anger in his every step. Glancing about, she could not blame him for being mad. The few head of cattle had done a lot of damage. When still fifty steps away, Dexter began his verbal assault.

"For crying out loud, woman! I've told you people a dozen times to keep those pests out of our fields! Look at what they did!"

"I'm sorry, Mr. Cline. Those stray steers wandered away from the main herd. We didn't realize they were missing until Billy cut their trail a little bit ago."

"Excuses don't replace the crops they ruined."

"We've been doing our best to watch them," Timony replied meekly. "This is the first time in a week or more that any of our cattle have come this far."

Billy returned at a lope and skidded to a halt next to Timony. He removed his hat and waved it back and forth, fanning his face.

"That old brindle steer is the culprit," he said, out of breath from the ride. "Every chance he gets, he leads a few of the others off and gets into trouble."

Dexter menacingly held up his rifle. "Maybe a bullet between the eyes would put an end to that."

Billy laughed, as if Dexter was joshing. "Old Briney—that's what we call him—is the best lead steer we've ever owned. Whether we have to run a few head or a whole herd, he's the one we put in the front. The other cattle follow him without a fuss, and he usually goes pretty much where we want him to. Makes him a valuable beef to keep around."

"Them cows of yourn have crossed the line for the last time, Fairbourn. I can't be letting them come in and stomp all over my crops every few days. I mean to figure a way to keep them out, even if I have to stand guard with a rifle twenty-four hours a day and shoot the first one to step into my field."

Billy still smiled at his threat. "Well, you know the cattle were using this for range, long before you and the other farmers come to the valley, Mr. Cline. Can't hardly expect them to recognize boundaries."

"I'm giving fair warning," Dexter maintained. "The line has been drawn. If them cows of yourn cross it one more time, they'll sure enough pay the penalty."

The smile faded from Billy's face. "I don't blame you for being a might put out, Mr. Cline, but you don't want to go shooting at our cattle for walking into a patch of your corn."

"Pass the word to John; you've been warned."

Timony reached over and touched her brother on the arm. "Let's go, Billy."

However, Billy turned his attention to Leta Cline, the eldest of the three sisters. He lifted a hand to tip his hat, a flirtatious smile curling his lips upward.

"It's good to see you again, Miss Leta. How've you been?"

Leta's complexion darkened, a red hue from the embarrassment of speaking in front of her brother, sisters, and father. Even so, she met his greeting with a delicate smile of her own. “I’m doing fine, William.”

“Sure do beg your pardon for the trouble our cattle caused your family.”

“They do try our patience.”

“Say good-bye, Billy.” Timony spoke up, aware that Dexter was fuming. She reined her horse around, nudged the mount with her heels, and set off in a lope. Billy raised a hand in farewell and hurried to follow after her.

Jimmy Cline directed the plow horse to stop next to where Dexter was standing. He waited until the Fairbourns were out of hearing distance before he spoke.

“Them cows done a heap of wreckage, Pa. What are we going to do?”

Dexter did not answer his question. Instead, he took another look around. “Save what stalks you can and pull them what is destroyed. I’ll be at the house.”

“Sure, Pa.”

Dexter took a step, but paused to stare at Leta. “Since when do you call Billy Fairbourn by his first name?”

“You remember, after the Christmas social last winter, you allowed that he could come calling and we could sit together at the Sunday meetings.”

“Don’t recollect saying he and you could refer to one another by your first names.”

“No, Pa.”

With an all-inclusive grunt, Dexter whirled about and started back toward the house.

"You ought to take advantage of the hot water you're in, Leta," June teased the oldest girl. "I'd say there's plenty for a bath."

"You're real funny, June," Leta gibed in return. "Funny looking, that is!"

Dexter kept walking, pretending not to have overheard their harassing back and forth. He was still boiling, but there was no need to bellow at the kids. The intruding cattle were not their fault.

In truth, he hated to get cross with the Fairbourn family. He liked them, especially John. A good many of the other ranchers went out of their way to give the farmers a hard time. Some had started fights and had even shot a milk cow or purposely driven their stock through newly planted fields. John had taken the position that there was room for all in Broken Spoke. It rankled some of the other ranchers, but he was fair-minded. More than that, he was the head of the Ranchers Association. Collectively the farmers all owed him a debt for keeping many of the other ranchers from causing trouble. Still, it was not enough.

Helen was at the door waiting. The wrinkles in her face and gray in her hair had changed her appearance over the years. She was not the same energetic, serious, and moderately attractive girl he had married twenty years ago. However, the youth and energy had been replaced with a pleasant maturity and inner beauty. She was more than mother and wife, she was his counsel, his adviser, and most of all, a friend he could rely on in any situation.

"Did they do a lot of harm, dear?"

"Tromped all over a half-acre or so. We probably lost a good portion of the crop on that end."

"I wish we had a couple dogs. They might keep the cattle from coming back."

Dexter took a moment to place the Henry rifle back on the rack above the door. When he looked at Helen, he knew she could see he had something in mind. It was a silent communication, the way either of them could often discern what the other was thinking.

"What is it, dear?" Helen asked quietly.

"I'm going to send a letter off to James. It's time we farmers quit being pushed around in this here valley."

"What can your brother do?"

"At our family gathering last year, he made a proposal to lend us a hand. I was hoping we wouldn't have to take him up on the offer."

The color drained from Helen's face. Fearfully she seemed to hold her breath. "You don't mean…"

Dexter sighed, resigned to the chore that lay ahead. "It's the only way left to us."

Helen wrung her hands, but she did not argue. Dexter had made up his mind. She knew his decision was for the good of the family. Even so, she was unable to shed the misgivings that rose to surface.

"Is there no other way?"

"None I can think of."

Without another word on the subject, she pivoted toward the freshly cleaned stove. "I'd better finish up with the stove and get supper started."

Dexter silently thanked the Almighty for such a woman. Even if his notions turned to mud, she would never censure his decision. No man could ask his wife for more than that.

Chapter Two

Luke Mallory sat upright, hat in his hands, barely breathing. For five long years, he had worked and sweated to get to this point. He had been snowbound and nearly froze in winter, wilted from the blazing heat of summer, and choked on the alkali dust of a thousand miles. He had battled his way through several holdup attempts and earned a reputation as a strong company man.

To get this far, he had never let up, hounding every agent at every Wells Fargo office to learn more about the business. He had worked on his off hours for free, studied at nights in his hotel room, anything to get a favorable word passed on to Sherman J. Porter. Finally, after all the months, his dedication and determination looked as if it might actually pay dividends.

Sherman had an unlighted cigar in the corner of his mouth. As he stared at the paper in his hands, his jaw muscles flexed, and he shifted the cigar from one side to the other.

"I've been hearing good things about you, Mallory."

"Thank you, sir."

Sherman leaned back, placing the paper onto the large desktop. He was a stately looking man, broad of chest, erect, with pork chop sideburns, a neatly trimmed beard, bushy eyebrows, and penetrating, chocolate-colored eyes.

"It hasn't escaped my attention that you have made several applications to become an agent for the company. I can tell you truthfully that your name has come up more than once for a station of your own during the past year or so." He gave a meaningful bite on the end of the cigar, as if to accent his point. "As you know, Wells Fargo and Company is the largest express operating in this part of the world. As such, we have some of the most qualified applicants in the country eager to work for us."

"I realize that, sir."

"We are growing bigger, adding services, and have something in the neighborhood of two thousand offices nationwide."

"Yes, sir. I've been to no less than a hundred doing stage and freight runs."

"We have a mind to open another agency over in Wyoming. You are on our list of possible agents for that position." He narrowed his gaze. "I, myself, will make the final determination."

"Yes, sir."

"It states on your record that you have no family?"

Luke fidgeted, shifting positions in the chair. "I always called Joe Boone my uncle. He took me in when my folks died of fever. I earned my keep cleaning stables and tending stock around his livery till I joined the Fifth Cavalry."

"Yes, two years with the Cavalry, and a short stint as a deputy under Bill Hickok." He narrowed his gaze. "The one they called Wild Bill?"

"Yes, sir."

He considered that and continued. "So you bounced around until you ended up driving stage for Wells Fargo."

"I began as a messenger, a guard on stagecoach runs. Once I learned to handle a team, I won a job hauling freight and sometimes driving stage."

Sherman appeared satisfied with his background. "I'm sure you know there is much more to being an agent than there is to being a driver."

"Yes, sir."

"An agent has to handle mail, purchase goods of every description, execute commissions of all kinds, make collections, and ship valuables to most any place in the world. You run a bank and a post office and are a shipping agent. It's a big responsibility."

"I'm aware of that, sir."

Sherman drummed his fingers lightly on the top of the desk. "You've made some friends along the way, Mallory. Several agents have recommended that I give you a chance at your own station. I do take their opinions into account."

Luke experienced a surge in expectation, but masked it. He had gotten his hopes up more than once and then watched the job go to another, better educated man.

Sherman was silent for a moment. The room was so quiet that Luke could hear his own heart pounding. He hoped Sherman didn't hear it too.

"I don't like to place conditions on something as important as appointing an agent, Mallory." Sherman leaned forward and removed the cigar from between his teeth. "But I have a chore that needs doing. There aren't but one or two men in the entire company to whom I would entrust this assignment."

A warning signal seeped into Luke's consciousness. He held his breath and waited for Sherman to continue.

"I'm of a mind to believe that you could handle the job."

"Yes, sir."

For the first time since their meeting, it was Sherman who appeared ill at ease. "I won't stir your coffee with a pitchfork; the task is a dangerous one. However, if you lend a hand with this situation, I would be inclined to approve your appointment."

Luke was attacked by a mixture of elation and dread. He had the job, but there was a condition. Instead of speaking, he waited for Sherman to spit out the details.

"The problem is this, Mallory. We have an order of barbed wire coming into Cheyenne tomorrow." He let the news sink in for a moment. "The wire needs to be delivered to Broken Spoke, Wyoming. There are a handful of farmers up there, trying to homestead right in the heart of cattle country."

A black storm cloud passed over Luke's head. He

felt the cold wind pervade his body. It was all he could do not to shiver.

"Barbed wire?" he repeated, hoping against all odds that Sherman had made a mistake.

"Enough for a full, double-wagon load. It has to be delivered by the end of the month."

"I see."

Sherman replaced the cigar. "Now, mind you, you don't have to do this job. If you decide the risk is too great, we'll fork over our profit and even go beyond our fees to send the cargo under armed escort."

It was difficult to speak with his heart lodged at the base of his throat. Rather than attempt it, Luke did not respond.

' 'I can assure you the company has been careful to keep news of this shipment as quiet as possible. With any luck, you can make delivery to Broken Spoke and be out of town before anyone is the wiser." Sherman leaned forward in anticipation. "What do you say?"

Luke might have asked the obvious question, as to whether refusal meant not getting the appointment as a new agent. He knew the amount of risk involved. More than one driver had ended up beaten or killed for trying to haul barbed wire into cattle country. However, his solitary desire in life was to be a Wells Fargo agent. If he had to face death to get the job, he would do just that.

"I'll deliver the wire, sir."

Sherman's face broke into a smile and he reached out across the desk. As Luke shook the man's hand, he could see the relief in his face. No doubt, he had been pressured to find someone foolish enough to make the haul. With the company's reputation of *we ship anything to any place* on the line, he had been desperate.

"Good luck, Mr. Mallory," he said, using a "mister" for the first time since meeting Luke. It was a sign of being on equal footing, a term of acceptance.

"I won't let you down, Mr. Porter."

"That's fine, my boy. Soon as you return from Broken Spoke, we'll get you trained and settled in your new job."

Luke said his farewell and left the room. The danger that lay ahead was overwhelmed by his exhilaration over the likelihood of his appointment. It didn't matter to Luke what the conditions, his dream was going to come true. He would soon be somebody, a Wells Fargo and Company express agent. With that title came respect and prominence in a community. He could hold his head up high, and for the first time in his life, he would be an important man.

"Only one thing between me and my destiny," he said to himself, "a trip to Broken Spoke with a load of devil's rope!"

Billy came through the back door as Timony was stoking the fire so she could put potatoes into the oven to bake. He gave a smirk at the bandanna she had tied around her head to keep her hair in place.

"That rag around your head makes you look like an old washerwoman."

"Thank you for the compliment. I hope you won't

be surprised when your potato is still raw in the middle."

He laughed. "I was only funning, Sis. Now that I take a second look, having that scarf wrapped around your head makes you look more like a housewife and mother."

"Goodness, how much better I feel about myself."

"Speaking of feeling good, we ran into Fess at the upper meadow this morning. He was digging the spurs into John about courting you again."

Timony groaned at the thought. Fess Renikie was fifteen years her senior, had greasy black hair that hung to his shoulders, and always had one protruding cheek from a sizable chaw of tobacco. He wasn't obnoxious, didn't smell or anything, he was simply not someone she enjoyed being around.

"What did John tell him?"

"He put him off, same as always, but it's getting a little embarrassing."

"What is?"

"The fact that you don't seem to have an interest in a single guy in the territory. You're twenty years old, and you've never taken a ride with a man, never let one escort you to a dance, never been on a picnic or anything."

"I haven't found one to my liking yet."

"You sure that's all it is?"

She cocked an eyebrow in a curious glance. "What's that supposed to mean?"

Billy had a rare moment of being serious. "We both grew up without a mother, Sis. You grew up looking after John and me, kind of like we were your responsibility. You not only help with chores, but you make sure the housework gets done, the laundry, the cooking and all. Maybe you are so busy tending and fussing for us, you don't feel you have time for another man."

"You've been out in the sun too long, Billy."

He gave his head a negative shake. "All I'm saying is, you don't have to spend your life taking care of us. You have a life of your own. Don't let it go to waste."

"I suppose you think I should offer Fess some encouragement?"

That put a grin back on his face. "I hope you never get that desperate for courtship." He was again his joking self. "Like I was saying, there are sure a lot worse things than picking up after your brothers."

"At least we agree on that."

Billy glanced about the table and counter. "Baked taters and what?"

"It won't be rabbit or venison," she answered. "You and John haven't shot any game in a month."

"I'd about dance barefoot in a nest of scorpions for the chance to get away and do some hunting. This roundup routine is killing me."

"We must be about finished. John let me come home yesterday."

"He's giving you a rest, because our coal pile is no bigger than an anthill."

"I hadn't looked lately."

"About time we start hauling fuel for the winter. I brought in the Shires so Token could shoe them."

"Sounds as if I've got a trip or two ahead of me."

"The team ought to be ready in a couple days. I'd be happy to make the trip, if you don't want to go. I haven't been to Rimrock since last Fourth of July for the big fair."

"Not this round," Timony said. "I can use the relaxation of a leisurely trip to Rimrock and back."

"Leisurely?" He grinned. "I've seen the way you drive the team."

"They enjoy the exercise."

"Yeah, but not nearly so much as you enjoy the speed of the wagon and the wind in your face."

"You better not tell John!"

"You think he don't know, Sis?" Billy gave her a soft punch to her shoulder. "Why do you think he prefers to let you make the trip? You always make it back by supper the next day. I don't often get home for two or three days."

Timony purposely gave a lift to her chin, raising her nose into the air. "See? That's the real difference between us. Big casinos don't hold any excitement for me. John knows I won't gamble or chase around all night like you do."

"A little fun—"

"And," she interrupted pointedly, "John has never had to pay a fine to bail me out of jail."

"One time!" Billy cried. "Besides which, it wasn't my fault. I thought the girl was old enough to be out late. She said it was okay with her father!"

"Let's not forget the money you lost. How much was it? Two hundred dollars?"

Billy threw up his hands in surrender. "Okay, okay! Like I was saying, Sis. I hope you have a good trip."

"There is one thing, Billy." She stopped him from leaving the room. "When the time comes to leave, I'll let you harness the team for me."

"How generous of you. I really enjoy strapping the shires in for a run I don't get to make."

"It's nice to know that I can always count on you."

"Yeah, right."

Luke picked up his team and made his way toward the depot. Even before he reached the railroad station, the hair felt as if it was standing up on the back of his neck. He was vigilant at once, eyes constantly moving, his rifle loaded and ready for immediate use. One mistake, one missed shadow lurking nearby, could mean a beating or even death. Most cattlemen were deadly serious in their efforts to prevent barbed wire from entering what they considered free range. He would have to be on guard at every turn.

No one appeared to be paying him any special attention, and he saw nothing suspicious, while directing his team of mules across town to the railroad station. Upon his arrival, he made a wide turn and pulled up next to the loading dock. He paused, short of breath at the sight. There it was, an entire platform full of barbed wire.

Frank Wanewright, the Wells Fargo agent from Cheyenne, was standing with a man Luke knew from the railroad. The two men appeared to be comparing notes, making certain the count was correct on the shipment.

As Luke stopped his tandem wagons in place, Frank glanced up and gave him a curt nod. Even that slight motion relayed the man's nervous apprehension. Luke set the break, tied off the reins, and jumped down to the ground.

The railroad man looked his way and grinned. "So this is the crazy coot you talked into taking the load of wire, huh?" He stopped what he was doing and moved over to extend a hand as he spoke. "Mallory, you've got to have a secret wish to be singing with the angels." He chuckled. "Come to think of it, hauling this stuff don't make it much of a secret anymore."

"Good to see you too, Deacon," he replied, shaking hands.

The man grinned at the nickname. "Don't have much time for preaching anymore."

"You call him Deacon?" Frank asked.

"A private sort of joke between the two of us," Luke explained. "I was riding on the train with him one time when a major storm hit. We were snowed in, miles from the nearest station, for a solid week. Burned every stick of wood we could find, including the benches and chairs out of the passenger cars."

"It was brutal," Deacon said, contributing to the story. "We were near freezing, the wind was howling through the cracks around the car windows, and kids were crying from hunger. I began to quote Scripture and pray. Next thing I know, everyone on the train is on their knees, praying right along with me."

"His doing or not, it worked," Luke told Frank. "A rescue crew arrived not an hour later. We were dug out and moving again by the next day."

"Worst time I ever had, since coming to work for the railroad," Deacon admitted.

"Made conductor at last, I see," Luke said, taking note of the man's uniform.

"And you notice the sweet run I ended up with? All the way to the end of the tracks and back as far as Kansas City to the stockyards. I don't exactly see those plush hotel cars like the ones George Pullman designed. On my runs, we bring in mostly supplies and a hoard of immigrants. The return trip is with cattle, pigs, sheep or, crops from the farmers or co-operatives. Real glamorous position I landed."

"Before the two of you start exchanging tales of family and friends," Frank interrupted, "how about we get this wire into the wagons and covered up before everyone in town sees it."

"Sure wish I could stick around and lend a hand," Deacon said, showing a smirk, "but I'm running a little behind. Got a schedule to keep, you know."

"We can handle it from here. Be seeing you, Deacon."

"You too, Mallory." He again showed a taunting smile. "Either in person, or at least in the obituary listings in the local news letter."

"Nothing like a vote of confidence to start a man on his way, Deacon. Thanks a lot."

"Godspeed, especially with your gun!" Thus Deacon ended their exchange. Then he was hurrying over to the train. He gave a signal to the man back at the caboose and waved the go-ahead to start rolling. With a cloud of black smoke and a squeal of iron wheels on iron tracks, the train began to move.

"Let's get at it!" Frank was ready to start loading. "I've got an ax handle that we can shove through the spools of wire. Shouldn't take us more than a few minutes to get you loaded up."

"Never knew you to be such a workhorse, Frank."

The man rotated his head about quickly, eyes searching the alleyways and windows of each and every nearby building. "You've got to be as crazy as a horse with a bellyful of locoweed, Mallory. I wouldn't haul this stuff across the street, let alone take it up into the middle of cattle country."

"I've got my reasons, Frank."

"Whatever they are, I hope they're worth dying for."

"I'm only a teamster for Wells Fargo; I'm not selling the wire. No need for anyone to get their hackles up because of me doing my job."

"You can't be that dumb. If you're caught with this load, you'll end up full of lead or hanging from the nearest tree. I'm not fooling you one bit. The last guy who took wire up into Wyoming was sent back wearing it. Tell you the truth, Mallory, them ranchers about killed him."

"Well, if it'll make you feel better, I don't intend

to advertise what I'm hauling this trip. I'll keep the load covered during the entire trip."

"The only thing I feel better about is the fact that you aren't going to leave a widow and kids behind."

Luke pulled out his buckskin gloves and slipped them on. "Knowing how much you care makes me all quivery inside, Frank."

"I'm the one doing the quivering. Let's get this bad news loaded before trouble shows up."

"Ready when you are."

Chapter Three

"I don't know how long you are going to be able to come courting, William," Leta told Billy. The concern shown brightly in her face. "After the way your cattle trod all over our corn, I'm surprised Pa let me go on this picnic with you."

He dismissed her concern with a wave of his hand. "It was only a few head that slipped away from the herd. Besides, we pushed them back far enough that they didn't come back for seconds."

"You know it won't be the last time. Every few days, we end up shooing off at least a cow or two."

"It's impossible to keep tabs on every straggler, Leta."

"Impossible or not, Pa has had his fill. He isn't going to stand by and allow it to happen again."

Billy chuckled. "Let me guess, you and your sisters are going to take turns guarding the crops. Did he make you some slingshots, or are you going to carry rocks and sticks?"

Leta set her teeth. "William, this is serious! Those

fields are our life. If we don't harvest a decent crop, we'll starve during the winter."

"Some choice, you either starve or exist on hominy, grits, corn bread, and a dozen other corn-based foods." He made a deliberate inspection of either side of her head and uttered a satisfied grunt. "Not yet."

She wrinkled her brow. "Not yet what?"

"From your eating all that corn, I was worried that you might have husks growing from your ears."

"How flattering."

"That's me, always a generous word."

"Okay, I admit that most of what we eat is made up of corn." Leta was no longer amused, her words becoming sharp and crisp. "We also have field corn to feed our cow, horse, and chickens. And we raise a little broomcorn for making brooms to trade at the general store for sugar or salt. Is that a sin?"

"Easy, gal." He realized her humor was gone. "Let's quit yapping about your corn." He attempted to laugh. "After all, the only corn that interests me is the one on my little toe."

"William!" Leta snapped harshly. "You can be a real boor sometimes!"

"What'I do?"

"We are in the midst of a potential range war, and you sit here and make stupid jokes!"

"Range war? What range war?"

"That's what is coming."

"Don't tell me you farmers are going to gather up your hoes and shovels and challenge us to a fight? Be about the same as a couple mice threatening a room full of cats."

"I'm not talking about us attacking you. If anyone is the aggressor, it'll be the ranchers."

"That's ridiculous. Why would we want to attack you?"

"Because of the wire!" she blurted out. "That's why!"

Billy had not taken much of her argument to heart, but the mention of wire removed all humor from his demeanor. He had been concerned as to how to do more than hold Leta's hand. Suddenly, the mood had changed.

"Wire?" he hissed the word vehemently. "Your pa is bringing in barbed wire?"

Leta recoiled, instantly repentant for letting the news slip. "William, you mustn't tell anyone!"

"Oh, as if it's going to be a secret!"

"I mean, Pa would know that I told you. I'd never get to see you again."

Billy was seething inside. *Barbed wire.* It was like mentioning the plague or smallpox. He no longer had an appetite for the bread pudding Leta had prepared. Ruefully, the thought of swiping a kiss was also a lost ambition. Such abominable news had to be shared with his brother as soon as possible.

"I'd better take you home," he said tightly. "Wouldn't want your pa to come looking for us."

Leta was crestfallen. "William, you do understand, don't you? We have to do something to protect our crops!"

He understood perfectly, at least, concerning the one thing she had told him. There was a range war coming.

John and Token were replacing the cracked whiffletree for the chuck wagon when Billy entered the yard at full gallop. Both men stopped work to see what was up.

"What's the rush, little brother?" John asked, noting that Billy's horse was lathered from a hard run. "Did Dexter catch you kissing his daughter?"

"Is Timony already gone?"

"An hour or so after you left this morning," John replied. "Why?"

Billy looked down the trail, leading away from the ranch. He swore under his breath and displayed a sour expression.

"Ain't no way we could ever catch her now, not the way she drives those shires."

"You should talk, Billy," Token put in. "She don't run them animals any more than you."

John regarded him a curious squint. "Why should we want to catch Timony anyhow? She'll be back tomorrow night."

"I think either you or I should have made this run, John."

"Why?"

"Yeah, what's going on, Billy?" Token was the one to ask. "You come a-riding in here like the devil himself had latched onto your saddle blanket."

Billy let out a deep breath and looked at the ranch

hand who had been the best man at the wedding of his mother and father. Token was more than a hand, he was like an uncle, a member of the family.

"Leta Cline let slip that there's some barbed wire supposed to be headed this way."

"What!" John exclaimed. "The farmers are bringing in wire!"

"She didn't say when, only that it was coming. I figured if you or I made the trip to Rimrock, we might get a line on it."

John automatically stared in the direction Timony had gone. "It's too late for that now, Billy."

"What're we going to do, John?"

"I'd say there ain't no question of what we do," Token broke in gruffly. "If them plow chasers plant a post, we yank it out. If they string even a single strand of wire, we cut it into tiny pieces and shove it down their throats!"

"The last thing we want is a war with the farmers," John objected.

"What else can we do?" Billy asked. "You remember how Pa and the others took care of the last shipment of wire to come into Broken Spoke!"

John's chest heaved with a deep sigh. "Yeah, and Pa died of apoplexy not a month later. It ain't only bullets that kill people, Billy."

"His death didn't have nothing to do with getting rid of the wire," Token said. "We got to stand tough on this."

"I sit at Sunday meetings with these folks, Token," John said. "My little brother is sparking a farmer's daughter. I've traded beef for corn to help them through the winters."

"You're as soft as cotton, John," Token told him, without a hint of condemnation. "Your pa always tried to do what was right and what was best for the ranchers. When we about had a fighting war because of Fielding bringing in his sheep, he give old man Fielding the chance to prove that his critters didn't destroy the land and pollute the watering holes." He gave his shaggy head a shake. "He was always willing to look at both sides, but not when it came to wire. He knew to act before the first post could be planted."

"Cline has to know that bringing in wire will start a bloody feud between the farmers and us ranchers," Billy said.

"I expect this is their last recourse," John surmised. "We haven't been able to keep our cattle from ruining a portion of their fields, and *we've been trying.* You can imagine how the farms have fared that are contiguous to the Renikie or Von Gustin ranches."

"Still, we got no choice, John," Token declared. "We sure can't sit back and let them string that razor wire across the range. They'll break our backs! We'll be ruined inside a year!"

"I don't think the farmers are that stupid, Token. They don't want to see their men beaten and killed, maybe a woman or some helpless kids too."

"I agree with Token," Billy said, "we can't sit back and do nothing."

John frowned in thought. He was the appointed leader of the Ranchers Association. Any action, or lack of action, would be on his shoulders. It was an awesome responsibility.

"So, what do you think, big brother?" Billy prodded him again. "How do we handle this?"

"Did your gal tell you when the wire was due in?"

"No, only that it was coming."

Token put his hands on his hips. "I'm still for taking a dozen men and going to look. We find the wire and send the driver packing, same as your pa and the Renikie boys done the last time."

"They could have killed that teamster."

"Sometimes it takes a little blood to make a point."

John turned his attention back to Billy. "If we can intercept the wagon, we could make sure the wire never gets delivered. You think Leta will tell her father about warning us?"

"I don't know. She didn't mean to tell me in the first place."

"We'll have to be prepared either way, Billy. I'll ride into town and keep an eye out for the wire. Let's keep a lid on this for the time being."

"All right, John. Whatever you say."

"How about the rest of the ranchers?" Token wanted to know.

John stared off in the direction Timony had gone. "There's nothing for any of us to do now but wait."

The dust was two inches deep on the well-traveled road. It boiled up from the churning hooves of Luke's team like a swirling cloud of steam. As he passed the turnoff to Broken Spoke, Wyoming, Luke emitted a loud whistle and cracked his bullwhip above the lead pair of mules, prompting them to speed up their pace. It was a full day to Broken Spoke, but only five or six miles to Rimrock. He could be there about sundown. The one thing he didn't want was to be caught out in the open at night. If word of the wire had spread, there might be any number of angry ranchers looking to catch up with him. It would be safer to hole up at Rimrock for the night.

Ominous clouds were forming off in the distance. Wyoming was not known for rain, but it looked like a storm was brewing. A little moisture would be welcome for dampening the powdery trail dust, but Luke did not relish getting wet. The impending rain was one more reason to spend the night at a boardinghouse or hotel, rather than roughing it out on the trail all night.

The sound of approaching horses reached his ears. He grabbed his rifle and whirled about.

A four-horse team and wagon appeared, charging up behind him at full-tilt. He spied a lone person atop the wagon seat, so he immediately relaxed and placed the rifle back down.

Before he could guide his mules to the side of the road, the outfit sped out into the brush and went flying around him. He spied a beautiful young woman at the helm, directing the animals as if born with reins in her hands! Once by him, she cut back onto the road so closely that his lead mules shied from the sliding wagon. The action from her spinning wheels and the flying hooves of her horses threw up a great cloud of dust. It swirled about and engulfed both Luke and his team.

"Hey!" Luke shouted after her. "What's the all-fired rush?"

Through the nebulous haze, he watched the wagon fishtail back and forth momentarily. The woman was clad in a buckskin skirt and light denim jacket, and he could make out her velvet black hair flowing wildly in the breeze beneath a jockey-style hat. With the knack of a professional teamster, she controlled the reins in one hand and wielded a buggy whip in the other. He couldn't be certain, but he thought he detected a mischievous giggle as she straightened out the rig and continued to blaze a trail toward Rimrock.

He smiled after her and waved a hand in front of his face to clear the infernal dust. It seemed that his heart picked up its pace as he watched her disappear up the road. It was a good bet that the gal either lived in Rimrock or she would be spending the night there. With a corroborating grunt, he decided to do some checking around. Barbed wire or not, he had a powerful inkling to meet that young lady in person.

Whenever Timony came to Rimrock she stayed at the Widow Myer's boardinghouse. There was a retired judge who lived at the house. Often, she would spend the evening passing the time in conversation with him. He was entertaining and colorful, with a thousand stories to tell. This particular night, he was out of town. So, after the evening meal, with nothing else to do, she wandered out onto the enclosed porch, stopped at the railing, and inhaled the fresh scent from the downpour of rain.

"Quite a storm," an unfamiliar male voice came from behind her.

Cocking her head to one side, she glanced over her shoulder. She hadn't noticed the man before. He had been lounging in one of the porch chairs, but now rose to his feet in gentlemanly fashion and stepped into the light.

She measured him at a couple inches shy of six feet in height, lean and weathered from the sun, as sturdy looking as if his body were constructed out of steel rods. He wore a clean, form-fitting black suit, white shirt, and string tie, with a flat-crowned Stetson tipped slightly to one side. Not fancy enough attire to be a gambler, but dressier than most cow punchers.

"I'm not in the habit of speaking to someone to whom I have not been properly introduced," she informed him curtly.

He turned his head from side to side, looked about, and sighed. "Never a busybody around when you need one." Then he touched the rim of his hat in a polite gesture. "I beg your pardon for being so forward."

"You one of those traveling drummers, a salesman?" she asked.

"I'm a teamster for Wells Fargo," he returned. "I'm headed for Broken Spoke tomorrow. The name is Luke Mallory."

"And I'm Timony Fairbourn. I came in from Broken Spoke this morning." Pivoting slightly toward him, she allowed a simper to play along her lips. "I believe I went around you on the way into town."

Mallory reciprocated with a natural smile. Not strikingly handsome, she still found the man enticing. He moved a bit closer and, in the dim glow of dusk, she perceived the way the golden specks about the iris of his hazel eyes sparkled with a restrained excitement. His gaze never left her face, but she felt that he had visibly inspected her body inch by inch.

"That's what you call it—going around?" His voice was silk, his chuckle as soft and smooth as the babble of a brook. "I thought I was being passed by a runaway locomotive from the Union Pacific railroad."

She sanctioned the corners of her mouth to lift a bit more and rotated to face the man squarely. Resting her elbows on the porch rail, she leaned back in a relaxed pose.

"When driving a herd of mules," she teased, "you should expect people to pass by you as if you were standing still."

"I reckon it ain't polite to differ with a lady," he countered her challenge, "but when it comes to pulling freight, I've found mules are stronger and more durable than most horses."

"And slower than a change of season!"

He chuckled. "I reckon they aren't the fastest critters afoot."

"My team is a shire mix, all of them sired by the same stallion. There's not a better team in the territory."

"I took a closer look at them over at the livery, Miss Fairbourn. As nice a draft team as I ever saw."

Timony studied him. His disposition surfaced as a mix of teasing and flirting. She crossed her arms and asked offhandedly, "Are you leaving for Broken Spoke first thing in the morning?"

"Yes, ma'am, got a load of farm supplies to deliver."

"Then perhaps I'll see you on the trail"—she displayed a demure smile—"at least, until I and my team pass you by."

"I can't think of anyone's dust I would rather follow, Miss Fairbourn."

"Good night, Mr. Mallory," she said, prepared to go in for the night.

The man offered her a final smile and a tip of his hat. "Yes, ma'am, it was a pleasure meeting you."

Chapter Four

Luke looked over each mule and checked its hooves for loose shoes or imbedded rocks that could cause a stone bruise. As always, he was careful in his selection of lead animals, aware of which ones worked together best. His troublesome mules he split up or used as a pole team, hitched next to the wagon tongue. That way, he could use his whip to keep them from acting up.

He stretched the stiffness out of his back and shoulders. It had been a restless night. After so many hours on the trail, he should have slept like a frog during hibernation. However, hauling a load of dynamite would have been preferable to barbed wire. This was one load he wanted to be rid of as soon as possible.

If not for the vision of Timony Fairbourn coming to invade his thoughts, he might have gotten no rest at all. Her subtle beauty had blotted his concern about the cargo for a time. Recalling their meeting, he paused to stare off into space. He envisioned her beguiling, leaf-green eyes, the inviting mouth that offered untold delights, lips that glistened with anticipation, the unconscious way she moved her nubile body, even the languid sound of her voice.

Sixty miles, bonehead! He reminded himself, trying to shake the young woman from his brain. He had to concentrate on the minimum twelve hours of hard running over hill and dale country that lay ahead.

"Keep your mind on your on job," he said to the jack he was strapping into place. "Ain't nothing going to stop me from getting my own station."

"When a man commences tuh talk tuh animals," a razing voice cut into his concentration, "it's time fer him tuh quit spending so much time with his mules. Next thing, you'll be sleeping next tuh one o' them."

Luke's hand dropped to his gun, but he caught himself before he looked foolish by drawing the weapon. He looked over his shoulder and discovered the liveryman a few feet away and managed a grin at his observation.

"I reckon you know that most men don't cuddle up next to their horses at night for companionship, friend. It's for the necessity of warmth."

"Where did yuh come in from?"

"South."

"The fellow looked at the covered wagons. "What yuh hauling?"

"Farm tools," he answered.

The fellow turned his head and spat into the dust. The distaste was obvious. "There ain't but a dozen or so farmers in all of Wyoming," he jeered. "Don't tell me they is going to buy two wagons full of equipment?"

"I don't know anything about that end of it. I'm only delivering the load."

The man thoughtfully rubbed his chin. "Funny time of year for buying tools and such, now that the tilling is done."

"I suppose."

"Yuh kind of slipped in without my knowing it last night," he said, eyeing the wagons again. "I would have put up yore team fer yuh."

"The mules and I are used to each other. It was no problem."

The man advanced a step closer and reached for the corner flap of the canvas.

"Keep your hands off the wagon!" Luke ordered.

"What?" The liveryman said, startled. "I didn't do nothing!"

Luke recovered quickly. "It took me an hour to get everything tied down. Might get some more rain today, and some of that stuff don't hold up to water worth a hoot."

The man backed away. "Sure, I know how it is."

"I've got to be going," Luke said to put an end to the conversation. He dug out a half-eagle and tossed it to him. "Probably see you on the way back."

"The man smiled at being paid twice what he would have charged. "Yeah, sure thing, and good luck on yore run."

Luke didn't say so, but he was beginning to think he might need more than luck. The liveryman could have only been curious, or he could be a spy for some of the nearby ranchers. He had shown that he didn't care for farmers, so he might have been watching for the shipment of barbed wire. Luke wasn't going to risk allowing the man to examine his load.

Moments later, he drove his team down the street toward the general mercantile. The previous night's shower had done a good job of dampening the earth. There were a few puddles, but it appeared that the weather would not be a factor for his journey. The sun was out and the sky was a dazzling blue. The late June temperature would likely climb into the mid-70s.

He spied Timony, impatiently watching, as a middle-aged man and a youth of about fifteen loaded coal into her wagon bed from a huge pile. She rotated in his direction at hearing the approach of his team and wagons. Luke noticed the way she appraised his six pairs of rather insignificant-looking mules.

Rolling the wagons to within a few feet of her rig, he pulled the team to a stop. Touching his hat in a polite gesture, he said, "Good morning, ma'am."

An impish smile curled the girl's sinuous lips. "Good morning to you, Mr. Mallory. It's fortunate that we had so much moisture last night. You won't have to digest so much of my dust today."

He smiled pleasantly. "Just watch the turns, Miss Fairbourn. The trail will be slippery until it has time to dry out."

"I'm an old hand at driving a team, Mr. Mallory."

The man walked over from the coal yard and cleared his throat to get Timony's attention. "Be done here in about fifteen minutes, Miss Fairbourn. You want that put on your account?"

"Yes, Mr. Brown, if you don't mind."

He gave an affirmative nod of his head and sauntered toward the store.

Timony visibly took a deep breath and once again stared up at Luke. He was unable to read what she was thinking, but there was an odd excitement in her eyes, alive, dancing like so many nimble sprites around a night fire. Her voice, however, was without emotion. "I'll see you on the road, Mr. Mallory."

"Yes, ma'am," he replied. "Hope you have a good trip."

With the young lady watching, Luke struck up his team. The animals surged forward, lurching in unison. The heavy-laden wagon creaked and began to roll. A second crack of the whip and the team broke into an easy trot.

Luke wondered if he should not have waited for Timony. It might have been polite to allow her to leave town ahead of him. He discarded the thought. There would be no cloud of dust from his mules, so such a courtesy was not necessary. Also, if he let her start out ahead of him, he might never see her again. By leaving first, he would get one final glimpse of Timony as she flew past him on the road.

A few minutes later, as those thoughts were still floating about in his head, he heard the sound of her approaching team. This time he was ready. He eased his mules over to the side of the road and allowed Timony and her load of coal to streak past without having to take to the brush. She flashed a somewhat mischievous simper as her big horses and wagon lumbered by him.

He smiled in her direction, then watched the distance widen between her team and his own. The shires would not be able to hold such a pace for long, but they aptly put him and his team a long way back. Resisting the temptation to crack the whip and urge more speed from his mules, he allowed them to continue their easy, ground-eating trot. He wasn't about to catch her prize team of horses.

The road between Rimrock and Broken Spoke had no real mountains but there were endless rolling hills that provided a good many grades to pull, and one fair-size stream to cross.

Timony knew the endurance of her team. She kept up a rapid pace for several miles, then slowed them to a walk. There was no need to push them to excess. She wondered how close the teamster would be at midday. If she should stop for a bite to eat, he might catch up. She smiled inwardly at the thought. Perhaps he would want to start up a fire and boil some coffee or something. It could give them a little time to visit.

As she topped the crest of a hill, she rose to her feet and turned to look back over her shoulder. There was no dust after the rain, but on the high ground she might catch sight of Mallory and his team. They were at least a couple hills behind, but—

The grinding sound was her only warning. Timony swung around as the front wheel suddenly came off. The wagon pitched forward and down! The axle dug into the ground with a violent jolt and sent Timony reeling. She made a desperate grab for the handrail, but missed. The jarring stop sent her flying over the frontward side of the wagon in a somersault. There was no time to react. She landed hard on the back of her head and shoulders. The breath was driven from her lungs and the world spun crazily before her eyes. It seemed miles away in the distance that the team ground to a halt. Timony's instincts were to roll away from the deadly wheels or horse's hooves, but a blackness swept over her. She couldn't breathe, had lost all power of movement, and was totally overcome by an ocean of darkness.

Luke topped a rise that gave him a view of the rolling terrain ahead. He was surprised to see Timony's wagon and team up the road. Something was wrong.

"Ye-hah!" he shouted, slapping the reins to encourage more speed out of his mules.

His first thought was that someone had been lying in ambush, waiting for him. They could have mistaken Timony and her load of coal for him and the wire!

However, as he drew closer, he could see the awkward tilt of the wagon and one wheel lying off to the side of the trail. Fear still knotted up his insides as he spotted the girl's unmoving form, sprawled alongside her rig.

Luke pulled back on the reins and called his team to a stop. He had the brake set and was on the ground before the wagons had ceased their forward movement. He sprinted past his mules, his heart hammering, his chest searing with dread. Many a good driver had ended up severely injured or died of a broken neck from a wagon accident.

Even as he slid to a stop at the girl's side, Luke felt a wave of relief. She was rolling her head back and forth, beginning to regain consciousness. He spied a canteen, hanging on the railing, next to the driver's seat, on the wagon. He quickly snatched it up, then sat down on the damp earth and gently lifted Timony's head up onto his lap.

The girl was not fully conscious. She moaned softly, but her eyes remained closed. Luke took off his bandanna, tipped the canteen, and wet one end. Raising her head up into the cradle of his arm, he used the moist corner to carefully trace a path along her forehead and down to her cheeks.

"Easy there, little lady." He spoke soothingly, so she would not wake up frightened. "Everything is okay. You're going to be fine."

Timony seemed calmed by the words. For a few moments, she relaxed, and he continued to mop the dust from her brow. Then, quite abruptly, she came fully conscious. Her eyes popped open; she stared right up into his face and jerked upward.

"Whoa!" Luke tried to calm her. "Careful, gal, you might have busted a spring or something."

Timony sat upright, obviously still somewhat dazed. The landing had left her skirt in disarray, exposing her legs nearly to her knees. She gathered her senses and quickly smoothed the material to cover herself.

"A chicken would strut for a week, if'n it had laid

an egg the size of the one on your head," Luke told her.

She reached back and touched the bump at the back of her head. "I'm…I believe I'm all right, Mr. Mallory."

"Quite a tumble," he replied. "That there wagon must have stopped like a calf hitting the end of a rope."

She glanced over at the wagon. "It did."

"Are you sure you're all right?"

Timony flexed her shoulders and made an effort to rise. Luke put a hand under either arm and lifted her to her feet. She stepped away at once, as if unaccustomed to having anyone lend her a hand.

"I'm okay now, Mr. Mallory," she assured him once more. "There was no warning before the wheel came off."

His eyes left her to take inventory of her team and wagon. "We might have to unload half the coal before we can raise the wagon bed," he said flatly. "There's a lot of weight to lift off of the ground."

Timony flicked her eyes at him. "Then you'll help me?"

"I surely wouldn't leave you stranded, ma'am."

"Gallantry is an admirable trait," she said softly. "I would certainly appreciate the assistance."

The chore was not a simple one. Luke used a piece of coal as the fulcrum for the lever and then used a stout pole he carried for such emergencies. With the pole under the axle, it allowed him enough leverage to lift the corner of the wagon.

Meanwhile, Timony wrestled the wheel around to the hub. As it weighed nearly as much as she did, it was a task to get it into place. She battled to line up the wheel, grunting from the effort.

"Get it higher!" she said, panting and rocking the hub up next to the axle. "It needs to go higher!"

As the lever was buried against the ground, Luke had to lower the wagon and set the fulcrum closer to the wagon. This time, he was able to lift the axle high enough to line up. Timony strained and labored, struggling with the weight of the wheel. After a few tries, it slipped back into place.

"There!" she gasped. "Finally!" And with those words, she sat right down on the ground, winded to exhaustion from the effort.

Luke hammered the locking pin back into shape and drove it home to secure the wheel. With a critical eye, he walked around and checked the wagon over.

"Looks like you're ready to roll again," he concluded.

As he gazed in her direction, Timony rose up onto her feet. There was a rapid rise and fall of her chest, but she maintained her aplomb. Steadfast, with a cool demeanor in her voice, she murmured, "I'm beholden to you, Mr. Mallory, for…"She seemed a loss for words. "For helping me. You are indeed a gentleman."

Rather than croak like a big frog with a full stomach, he gave a subtle lift to his shoulders. "I never knew my ma, but I reckon she would have expected no less of her son than to lend a hand to a lady in distress."

"You would have made her proud."

For a long moment, Luke stood there, awkward, not knowing what else to say. He finally took hold of the brim of his J. B. Stetson and tugged downward in a polite gesture.

"Good day, ma'am. Keep an eye on that wheel."

Timony rewarded him with a bright smile. 'Thank you again, Mr. Mallory."

Before he could reach his mules, the young woman was back aboard her wagon. She cocked her head to the side and smiled at him a last time. The action sent his heart to pounding.

Luke stood, as if in knee-deep mud, still breathing hard from the recent exertion. As the shire team disappeared over the crest of the hill, he sighed. ''Luke, old boy," he muttered aloud, "that there is one special lady."

Timony let the team pick their own pace, sightlessly staring at the road ahead. She was lost to her own contemplation, assailed by sensations that were completely foreign to her.

For years, she had envisioned how it would feel to be held in her mother's arms. She had dreamed of gazing up at her mother's face and sensing the enjoyment and rapture of being pampered and loved. It came as a shock that she would have the same tender feelings, when the face she looked into had been that of Luke Mallory!

She squirmed from discomfort. She had been mollycoddled by a man. He had mopped her brow with a damp cloth and cradled her in his arms like a child. The benign murmur of his voice had soothed her fears and comforted her in a way she had thought only a mother could.

As if drawn to the teamster, she twisted about and looked back over her shoulder. He was not in sight. She was probably miles ahead of his slower team of mules.

If only Token didn't maintain our wagons, she thought. It would have given her an excuse to go into town, then wait around while the axle was checked and any repairs were made. Luke would arrive before the wagon was finished, and she would have a chance to see him again.

Timony admonished herself at the idea. What was wrong with her? She was considering literally throwing herself at a near perfect stranger! Did she have no shame?

The ache deep inside was something she had never experienced before. It was a hunger, an appetite for something unnamed. Awaking in his arms, it was as if all the yearning for her mother had been forgotten in a single instant.

But he isn't my mother! she told herself, annoyed that she would even compare a moment in Luke's arms with the endless yearning for a mother she had coveted for years. Regardless, the pang was real, and it wasn't only her tummy making a request for food.

"Land sakes, Timony!" she said through clenched teeth, "get your saddle on straight! You're mooning over that freighter like a love-starved kitten!"

Chapter Five

Broken Spoke was a few buildings, mostly sod with false fronts. There were several shops, a saloon, a few houses, and a fair-size barn and livery stable. Luke drove the team down the center of town and pulled up at the front of the barn.

"Say, howdy!" a man's voice cackled behind Luke. He rotated around to face a scrawny old man. He was as thin as if he were made out of sticks; gray whiskers hid the lower half of his face, and the bushy brows appeared to be all that kept his floppy hat from sliding down over his brightly shining eyes. His clothes were shabby but clean, his boots were scraped raw from lack of polish or oil, and he carried with him the scent of horses.

"Howdy to you too," Luke said, climbing down from his wagon.

"Bufford Jermiah Jones," the gent announced, extending a gnarled paw. "Everyone calls me Bunion."

Luke gave the hand a quick shake. "I'm Luke Mallory. You the liveryman?"

"I tends them all, sonny—horses, cows, sheep,

even a few pigs on occasion. I've holding pens for shipping about anything on four legs."

"Reckon I need a couple days' boarding for my mule team. They've been on the road for a week."

"You brung in the load of wire?"

Luke cast a nervous glance about. "How did you know that?"

"My pal runs the telegraph. He told me about the order being sent."

"Well, you heard it straight. I have a load of barbed wire for a man named Cline."

"That's going to liven up the valley some. Yup, you can bet your long-handles on it."

"I heard a rumor that there are some who resent barbed wire in Broken Spoke."

Bunion chuckled. "Resent is too tame of a word, sonny. The first old boy who strung wire was run out of the country. The last fellow who brung in a load of wire was bound up in a few strands and dragged about a mile out of town. He and the wire were shipped back to Cheyenne. That was about a year back."

"I've been told that tale, but I didn't know it took place here in Broken Spoke."

"It was mostly the doing of the Renikie brothers, but all of the cattlemen supported the action."

Luke took a careful look around and licked his lips, which were suddenly dry. "I didn't figure bringing wire up here would be real popular, but I don't have a personal stake in the local politics. I haul freight, that's it."

"You best hope Cline and the other farmers come to settle for your load real quick, sonny."

"Soon as I put up the mules, I'll see about contacting them."

"Don't worry about your animals," Bunion said. "I'll take good care of them."

"Is there some place I can get a room for a night or two?"

"Jack Cole, he's the pal I was speaking about, at the telegraph office. He's also our sometimes city marshal. He has a room he rents out. It's right up the street."

"Thanks."

"Come on along, sonny," Bunion offered, "and I'll introduce you." As they started up the street, he continued to talk. "Jack Cole uses a cane to get around, and he don't ride horses a'tall. He was working for the railroad, when a timber support at a bridge building site fell on him and crushed his right foot and ankle. He now runs the telegraph office and does some barbering. He ain't never married, but he does have himself and a mangy cat to care for."

As Bunion and Luke approached, Cole was sitting on the porch, leaning his chair back against the building's false front. When he saw that the two men were coming his way, he rocked forward and got to his feet.

"This be Luke Mallory, a teamster for Wells Fargo," Bunion said to introduce him.

"You must be hauling the wire," Cole said in lieu of a greeting.

"I'd rather not announce it to the world," Luke

said. “I don’t think I’d look good in a suit made out of that wire.”

“He needs a room for the night.”

“Shore thing,” Cole said, showing a friendly smile. “Step into my parlor and I’ll show you the cell….” widened the smile, “I mean the room.”

“It *is* a cell,” Bunion clarified, “but it don’t get a lot of use.”

Upon entering the outer room, a scruffy-looking gray-and-white cat appeared. It had long, matted fur, except for several nearly bald patches that were right down to the hide. Luke concluded that when Bunion had called it mangy he had been too kind.

“Where you been, Harlot?” Cole snapped at the cat. “I seen a mouse scooting across the floor like he owned the place this morning. Go catch it and earn your keep!”

“You named your cat Harlot?” Luke asked.

“Yeah, and for good reason, Mallory. Every tom in the area comes courting. You don’t think I took a set of shears to that moth-eaten ball of fur? It’s from her and the toms mixing it up. She’s got no class at all, no dignity, and I’m right certain she don’t have the word *no* in her cat vocabulary.”

Luke chuckled. “Must be a real shortage of female cats around. That’s about the ugliest critter I ever seen.”

“Been with me for ten years,” Cole replied. “A wagon run over her when she was only a kitten. It must have done something to her production faculties, cause she never has bore no kittens. That there's about the only thing good I got to say for her."

Harlot decided to investigate the newcomers and sauntered over to rub up against Luke's leg. He frowned at the number of white and gray hairs that immediately clung to his trousers.

"Likes you," Cole deduced, " 'cause you're a male. She don't hardly ever rub up to no woman."

"I suppose I should be flattered," he said dryly.

"The intros is done," Bunion said. "I'm heading back to the stable, before that scabby fur-ball starts to cover me with hair."

"Run, you coward," Cole taunted.

As soon as he was out of the room, Cole put a steady gaze on Luke. "Run into any trouble hauling the load of wire?"

"I've been lucky to this point."

"I've done my best to keep it quiet. I sent the message for Dexter Cline some weeks back. His brother is a banker or something, over in Denver, Colorado. Dexter got some financial help from him."

"I brought in five ton, still loaded on the wagons."

"I'll get word to Dexter soon as I can. You might want to make yourself scarce until delivery."

"Bunion mentioned that there was pretty strong opposition to stringing wire in this part of the country."

"Probably told you about the farmer, a couple years back, that brought in enough for his field of corn. That fellow ended up moving, after his house and fields were burned to the ground."

"Don't you have any law in these parts?"

"Maybe once we become a state, there will be real law in every town. Until then, most places are like we are. Shucks, I don't have no real power. I was given the badge by the mayor, so we could handle the cowboys on Saturday nights. If there was a murder or something, we'd have to ask the territorial governor for help and have them send a circuit judge to work the trial."

"All I want is be rid of the shipment of wire. If someone has a gripe, it ought to be between them and the ones who ordered the stuff, not with me."

"It don't work that way," Cole said. "The idea is to punish anyone who comes in contact with the wire. I've been half afraid they would come after me the next time."

"Why you?"

"For sending for the wire in the first place. Like I says, these ranchers are real narrow-minded when it comes to that devil's rope."

"How about that room?"

Cole glanced out the window and the color left his face. When he looked back at Luke, his expression displayed a mix of alarm and dread. "John Fairbourn," he whispered.

"Fairbourn?" He said, suddenly experiencing a sinking sensation. "He any relation to Timony Fairbourn?"

"Her brother, and head of the Ranchers Association."

The Ranchers Association: The words hung over the room like an ominous storm cloud. Luke didn't have to ask for any further clarification. He knew he was the one John was looking for.

"I saw him come to town yesterday. I'd say he's been waiting for you to show up, son."

Luke didn't have to ask if Cole would help. With his twisted foot, the man had a tough time walking under his own power. He wasn't likely to intervene. With a heavy sigh, Luke removed his buckskin gloves from his back pocket and slipped them on. He did not relish the idea of a fight, but he was going to be prepared. Too many men busted their knuckles on someone's teeth during a fight. Even if he won, the damage could maim the winner for months or even years.

"You the teamster?" John asked without emotion as Luke stepped out onto the porch.

"That's right."

John appeared to look him up and down, while Luke measured Fairbourn in return. About equal in height, John had about a thirty-pound advantage in weight. His arms were a bit longer and he had powerful-looking shoulders. The eyes were half-lidded as he studied Luke.

"I'm John Fairbourn," he announced.

"Luke Mallory," the teamster reciprocated. "I believe I met your sister in Rimrock. A wheel come off her wagon on the trail this morning."

John displayed surprise at the news. "You give her a hand, did you?"

"Seemed like the proper thing to do. She's quite a gal, John."

"I'm obliged to you for looking out for her."

"Long trip for a woman alone," Luke replied. "Might want to consider sending someone along with her next time."

"Timony has made that run a dozen times without incident," John told him. "She'd be real put out if I was to make her take along an escort."

"I agree she's as capable as any woman I ever met."

John took a deep breath, appeared to hold it briefly, then let it out slowly. "You know what I'm here for?"

"I've an idea."

"This is cattle country, Mallory. There ain't but a few farmers in all of Wyoming Territory. Know the reason how come?"

Luke shrugged. "Not much water for growing, I suppose."

"It's range country," John went on. "The land will accept a little hay, oats, or wheat, but that's about all. You know why that is?"

"I reckon you're going to tell me."

John remained both calm and patient, as if he was explaining about the stars and moon to a small child. "It's because those crops are needed to support cattle. One might think it likely that Wyoming was set aside by the Almighty, just for raising cattle."

"Do tell."

John took a moment to remove his gun belt and hang the pistol over the saddle horn of his horse. When he turned back toward Luke, there was a dark light of anticipation shining in his eyes.

"Once again, I'm obliged to you for looking out for Timony. I mean that sincerely."

Luke felt his senses come to life. His heart accelerated at a rapid pace, pumping adrenaline into his system. There was nothing to say, no way to avoid what was coming. He gave a sigh of resignation, unbuckled his gun belt, and placed it on a chair nearby. As he turned back around, he was aware that a number of people had gathered to watch.

"I'd admire for you to get your wagonload of wire and head back for Rimrock," John spoke again. "It would save me putting you into the wagon and doing it myself."

"Sorry to cause you any trouble," Luke replied, "but I have a delivery to make."

John raised his bony fists. "Always like to give a man a chance to save himself from a beating."

Luke raised his own fists. "You're a real decent human being, John."

The two of them moved into the street. After sizing up one another for a full circle, they came together like two bulls butting heads.

Luke ducked a blow that went over his shoulder, but was blinded by a jab to his right eye. He launched a right to John's ribs, bobbed back and forth, then jolted the man with a solid shot to his nose.

There came shouts from the onlookers, most of them in support of John. He responded by going on the attack. A flurry of punches came at Luke like a downpour of hail. He blocked or evaded a good many of them, but a few got past his guard. Rocked by a couple shots, he backed away, covered up, then countered with a blizzard of his own.

Bright lights blinded him from a punch to the side of his head. Before he could shake it off, he tasted blood from a set of knuckles that hit him in the mouth. He absently wondered if John had cut his knuckles on his teeth. Striking back again, he landed a pile-driving right to John's jaw. It staggered the man backward, but he did not go down.

Luke attempted to follow up the advantage, hammering away with everything he had. He sent punches flying, scoring a few good hits, but was unable to knock the man down. John was like a willowy tree, bending before the force of a gale, yet rebounding immediately as soon as the wind let up.

Luke had been a fighter all of his life and considered himself pretty handy with his fists. He figured he was doing pretty well, until he discovered his face planted against the damp earth. He shook the cobwebs from his brain, somewhat surprised at being flat on the ground.

"Crawl for your team of mules, teamster." John's voice was passive and controlled. "Take your wire and git."

Luke pushed himself back onto his feet and came up in a crouch. He spat a trace of blood into the dirt. "You got first bite of the sandwich, but you ain't eaten my lunch yet, Fairbourn."

There was blood smeared under John's nose and his one eye was puffy and nearly closed from swelling.

Even so, the man grinned. "You're game, wire drummer, I'll give you that."

"I know a woman in Cheyenne who can hit harder than you, and she's sixty years old."

John chuckled at Luke's spirit. "Good thing I'm only fighting you, Mallory, and not that old woman."

The two of them came together again, both swinging for all they were worth. Luke felt solid contact from a right hand. He risked a glance to see if it had done any damage….

The dark, moist earth was against his face once again. He lifted his head and wiped the dirt off of his chin. The world was spinning before his eyes, and there was no strength left in his arms.

"You getting the idea here, freighter man?" John asked. "I can do this all night."

Luke struggled back until he was sitting on his heels and groggily peered up at John. "Hah!" he said and snorted confidently, "you're so near being beat that you're all blurred and out of focus. Soon as the world stops whirling around, I'm going to fix your wagon so the wheels don't roll."

"You're beat, Mallory. Give it up."

Luke gave his head a negative shake. "I ain't leaving until I make delivery, Fairbourn."

"Do I have to kill you, to get through that thick skull? We ain't letting you bring wire into Broken Spoke!"

Luke surged upward, finally standing on his feet again. He lifted his fists to a point even with either side of his chin. He swayed uncertainly and stared hard at his adversary. His vision remained distorted, but he shook it off.

"Just 'cause there's three of you, don't mean you can whip me, Fairbourn."

John had his hands on his hips. He rotated his head back and forth and heaved a sigh. "You and my sister really ought to have gotten on well together. You're both as stubborn as the worst jackass ever born!"

Luke blinked against the blackness that threatened to overcome his awareness. From the heavy block upon his shoulders, it felt as if someone had replaced his head with an anvil. There was no strength in his arms, and his legs were wobbling under his weight. With more courage than sense he snapped, "You going to talk or fight?"

John took a step toward him. Luke tried to throw a right hand, but the change in his balance caused him to fall forward. He landed on his hands and knees, once again staring at the ground. He was gasping for air, searching for energy. He wasn't beat yet. If only he could muster enough strength to get back up, he could still win this fight.

John passed by him, walking to a nearby watering trough. After rinsing the blood from his face and hands, he returned to stand over Luke. In such an exposed, helpless position, the man could have kicked Luke in the head or broken his ribs. He did neither.

"Think about it, Mallory." John's words held no more emotion than when the fight had started. "Your load of wire will sure enough start a range war between the ranchers and the farmers. We don't want that here in Broken Spoke."

Luke tried to summon up a reply, but he was too fatigued to speak. After a few moments, he heard the sound of the man's horse as he rode back out of town. The fight was over.

Chapter Six

Timony jerked back on the reins to stop the team in front of the Fairbourn ranch house. She shoved the brake into place and jumped to the ground. The quick action caused a lightness to rush to her head.

"Hi, Sis," Billy greeted her, coming out the door. "You made good time. Didn't expect you back until well after dark." He noticed the way she was swaying uncertainly.

"What's the matter?"

Timony regained her senses and reached up with a hand to tenderly finger the bump on her head. "I had a little accident."

Billy was immediately concerned. He hurried over and looked her right in the eye. "What happened? You all right?"

"The front wheel came off and sent me flying tail-over-tin-cup." She lightly rubbed the back of her head. "I landed pretty hard."

Billy moved in behind her and examined the bump. "Lucky you landed on your head," he said, "or you could have hurt yourself."

"Thanks so much."

Satisfied that she was not hurt seriously, Billy stepped back in front of her. "You see John in Broken Spoke?"

"I didn't go into town," she answered. "What is John doing there?"

"We got some bad news, the day you left for Rimrock. Cline has sent for a load of barbed wire. It's likely to arrive at any time."

"Barbed wire!" Realization slapped Timony like a wet towel in the face. Mallory had told her he was carrying farm supplies!

"John is keeping an eye out for the stuff."

Timony was crushed and angered at the same time. She turned her back toward Billy and leaned forward slightly. "Kick me, would you? Hard!"

Her brother laughed. "What the duce are you talking about, Sis? Why should I kick you?"

"For being a stupid moron!"

"What's gotten into you, Timony? What are you talking about?"

Timony felt a burning heat rise up from her throat, but she seldom kept secrets from Billy. "I lost a wheel, on the road from Rimrock, a mile or so before Salt Creek. A teamster came along and helped me get the wheel back on."

"Let me guess, the one hauling the wire for Cline?"

"I didn't know he was carrying wire!" She was heated to fury. "He was a perfect gentleman. The fall knocked me cold, and he…" She stopped, unable to find the words to describe what had happened.

"He what?"

"I told you," she said, dismissing the personal treatment, "he helped me get the wheel back on my wagon!"

Billy shrugged his shoulders. "All right, so the old boy played the role of a gentleman. He's still bringing the wire to Broken Spoke!"

"What's that?" Token had come from the yard and overheard her final words. "The barbed wire! It's here?"

"I imagine it's reached town by now," Timony answered him. "The teamster's mules were making pretty good time. I doubt that I beat them here by more than an hour or so."

Token looked at Billy. "You think John can turn him back?"

"What are you talking about?" Timony was appalled. "You mean that's why John is in town?"

"He said he would stop delivery," Token informed her. "What's this teamster like? Think John can take him?"

"You mean in a fight?"

Token was taken back at her attitude. "He's with the farmers, Timony."

Luke Mallory is only hauling freight," Timony defended him. "He works for Wells Fargo."

"We don't have a choice, Sis," Billy said. "If the guy delivers the wire to the farmers, we'll be in for a fight."

"Billy brought us word of the wire the day you left,

Timony," Token said. "The Cline girl let it slip. It was too late to catch up to you."

"What is John going to do about it?"

"I expect he'll try and talk your teamster pal out of making his delivery."

"I don't think he is the sort of man to be intimidated, Token."

Token considered her response and then turned his attention to Billy. "You best ride over and tell Rob we're having a meeting of the cattlemen. Pass the word to Fielding too. His sheep need the open range as much as our cattle."

"All right, Token. When and where?"

"Make it for tomorrow morning, here at the house."

"I don't like the sound of this," Timony said, fearful of impending trouble.

"I'll unload the coal and put up the team," Token told her quietly. He gave her a quick once-over. "You probably want to rest up a bit and maybe take a bath."

Timony was desperately worried about what John had in mind, but she dared not take a horse and ride to Broken Spoke. John was the head of the family, the one in charge. He was the strongest physically and mentally, the eldest, and it was his duty. She held her tongue, intrinsically fearful of what action he might take.

Without another word, she walked around to the house and went inside. The interior was dark, compared to the bright light of the afternoon sun. Even though the Fairbourn home was one of the very few made of logs in Broken Spoke, it had only three windows for the main part of the house. Their home had a kitchen, sitting room, and two bedrooms, large and comfortable, when compared to the one-or two-room shanties of the farmers.

Timony had shared a room with both John and Billy, when she was young. After the death of her mother, John roomed with their father. When he passed away, John and Billy shared the main bedroom and she was given the privacy of her own room.

Entering the tiny cubicle, she closed the door behind her. The curtain was drawn over the only window, shutting out the late afternoon sun. The lamp was seated on a shelf by the entrance, but Timony did not wish for more light. She crossed over and sat down on her bed.

Unconsciously she reached over to the dresser and picked up her childhood doll. Not a baby in a nightgown, the doll had the mature face and dress of a young lady. She vaguely remembered John bringing her the doll when she had been sick with fever. Oddly, it was the same fever that took her mother's life. She might have grown to dislike the toy, relating its arrival with the death of her mother. However, it was quite the opposite. She adopted the sweet likeness as her best friend, a confidante whom she used to console her whenever her mood was dark.

Staring at the familiar doll, she beheld that some of the colors had faded or been rubbed from the wood-sculptured face. The hair had come from a horse's tail, and strands of it had been lost, causing a bald spot above one ear. As for the clothes, the satin and lace dress was worn and tattered with age, and the shoes had long since been lost. Still, it was Timony's most prized possession. She felt awkwardly childish, holding the doll close, but deep inside, she suffered a longing to be comforted.

Propping up her pillow in front of the dresser, she reclined against it and closed her eyes. A vision immediately formed to invade her tranquillity. The teamster appeared, cradling her in his arms, peering down at her with all the worry and anxiety of a parent.

"Curse your rotten hide, Luke Mallory!" she snapped aloud. "Why did you have to bring that vile barbed wire to Broken Spoke?" Cuddling the doll in her arms, she rocked back and forth slowly. "Why, why, why?"

Chapter Seven

Timony realized her worst fears at seeing John enter the room. There were rust-colored stains of blood on his shirt, his one eye was swollen shut, and his lower lip was puffy.

"I knew it!" she lamented. "You got into a fight with that teamster!"

John did not deny it. "Quite a fellow you found there, Timony. I whupped him to within an inch of his life and the sorry jack wouldn't quit."

"John! he helped me with my wagon! He could have left me stranded!"

Her brother gave her an innocent look. "I thanked him for it."

"Oh, you did!" She could not keep her voice from raising several octaves. "That should have given you a clear conscience while you beat him to death!"

John waved a hand to dismiss her concerns. "He'll be okay. He fought me fair and square, so I was careful not to break any of his bones."

"How thoughtful of you!"

"What's the matter with you?" he asked. "You soft on that freighter or something?"

"All I'm saying is that's a fine way to repay someone for his help!"

"We done covered that already," her brother returned. "You sure there isn't something more?"

It was Timony's turn to balk. "More?"

"I'm beginning to think you haven't told me everything. What happened out there betwixt the freighter and you that you ain't told me?"

Timony reared back defensively. "I don't know what you're talking about. Nothing else happened!"

"Look me in the eye and say that, Timony."

"I'm not a child, to be spoken to in such a way, John. You can either take my word or go suck on a spoiled egg!"

John took on a smug expression. "That teamster got to you, didn't he? That's it, ain't it?"

Timony whirled about and stormed quickly toward the kitchen. "I'll put your food on the table, John. It's stone cold, but that shouldn't matter to you. It'll match your heart!"

Dexter Cline waited until all of the farmers had arrived. Tom Kensington and Miller Queen were looked up to as spokesmen. He checked to make certain that everyone was present before he told the men the news.

"Wire is here," he said quickly, "five ton of it sitting down at the livery."

Some exchanged nervous glances, others took deep

breaths and exhaled slowly. Tom rubbed the stubble on his chin and said, "You think we can really get away with this?"

"We need that wire to survive," Cline told him. "We've got everything we own tied up in our farms. We have the right to survive."

"How about the Ranchers Association?" Tom queried. "You know they won't let us string wire without a fight."

"There was a fight already," Miller replied. "John tried to run the wire-hauling teamster out of town, but the guy wouldn't go. My boy, Dory, he seen the fight. That freighter wouldn't quit. John knocked him down several times, but the guy would not give up the fight."

"Glad Wells Fargo sent a man who stands his ground," Cline said. "We spent good money on that last load of wire and didn't get a single strand for our trouble."

"Me and my boys are ready," Miller said. "Dory and Chad been cleaning their rifles. We ain't going to back off no more."

"I guess I'm ready too," Tom added his consent. "I wish there was another way, but we've got to do something to protect our crops."

Cline looked over the room. All of the farmers were in agreement. Of the spokesmen, Tom was the weakest. However, once the war started, he would stick. Miller Queen and his two boys could be counted upon for muscle. They were a rough and tough family. As for his own kids, he had never been able to get his only boy out from under their mother's wing. Of his four children, Leta had the most savvy, but she was a girl. Worse, she was being courted by Billy Fairbourn. How he envied Miller for having tough, ready-to-fight sons.

"Let's get our wagons," he said finally. "We need to get that wire distributed before the cattlemen get organized enough to try and stop us."

Luke opened his eyes. The rays of light filtered through the cracks in the curtained windows. He lay there for a few minutes, staring at the ceiling. Not fully awake, yet unable to sleep. Oddly enough, his mind conjured up the image of Timony Fairbourn. He was lifted at the possibility of seeing her again. Under the right circumstances, he might one day kiss her inviting lips. Once he was an agent for Wells Fargo, he would be respected and important. She was bound to be impressed. If only he could get this job out of the way.

"You ever going to climb out of that bunk?" A grating voice brought Luke crashing back to earth. He rolled his head to one side to see the liveryman standing at the doorway.

"What time is it?"

Bunion grunted. "You ought to be asking what day is it." He gave his grizzled head a shake. "Way you fought against John Fairbourn, I figured you for the same stamina as them mules of yours."

"I must be getting old," Luke admitted, stiffly rising up onto his elbows.

Bunion scrutinized him for a few seconds. "You

ain't pale as the driven snow, you ain't been coughing up blood, and I don't see no bones sticking out through the skin. John took it easy on you."

"Right," Luke said cynically, "I feel as spry as if I'd been trampled by a herd of buffalo."

"You gave him what for there for a time. Not bad for a dude."

"I'm no dude."

Bunion uttered a grunt. "Well, then, you didn't do near so good."

Luke swung his legs over the edge of the bed and managed a sitting position. There didn't seem to be a muscle or inch of his body that didn't ache.

"This the room Cole was going to rent me for the night?"

"Nope, this here be my humble abode. I'm the straw-doc in Broken Spoke, so I brung you here to check you over."

"You're a doctor?"

Bunion straightened his shoulders. "Is that so hard to believe?"

"Odd combination, liveryman and doctor."

"I done most of my tending to stock, 'cepting for a hitch during the war. As some considered me past my prime, they stuck me in a medical corps, treating Yanks and Rebs alike. There is a midwife or two about to help with delivering babies, but I do most everything else."

"Sounds as if I'm in capable hands."

"Durn tootin', Mallory. You're lucky to have me around."

"Any word from Cline?"

"I risked my neck helping you already, Mallory. How much do you want for nothing?"

"Didn't mean to sound ungrateful."

"No matter, Cole sent word out to Cline this morning. I suspect he'll be coming in pretty soon."

"My thanks, to both of you."

"Sure, 'less John Fairbourn comes looking for me. A lot of good your thanks will do then."

Luke took a moment to evaluate the physical damage to his body. Everything seemed to function, although his facial muscles ached with any expression or movement. He gingerly moved his jaw back and forth and was relieved that everything worked. Even his teeth were intact, although a couple on one side felt a trifle loose.

"I do believe John trimmed my branches."

"He took it easy on you. Once he had you dazed, he could have chopped you into firewood. You best get your money and make tracks out of Broken Spoke. If it comes to a shooting war, you might be one of the targets for the Renikie brothers or Tito Pacheco."

"Pacheco?"

"Yeah, you might have heard of him. Reputed to be a bad man with a gun."

"He's a cattleman?"

"The Fairbourns and Renikie boys are. Tito is a hired tough on Fielding's payroll. Fielding has about twelve thousand head of sheep."

"Now that's a first for me, a gunman working for

a sheepman, and them hand in hand with the cattlemen."

"Two of Tito's cousins work for Fielding. Thanks to old man Fairbourn, afore he died, there never was any trouble between the sheep and cattle around here."

"Thought sheep ruined the pastures and water holes for cattle."

"Guess it don't have to work that way. Cows don't mind sharing the watering spots with the sheep and, so long as the sheep ain't allowed to overgraze, the grass comes right back up. You might say the cattlemen and Fielding have come to terms on the range."

"But the farmers are not invited to the party."

"They want to fence off water holes for irrigation and cut out big chunks of land with their wire. Tell you straight, it's going to end up with blood being spilled."

"There ought to be room for all three factions. Wyoming is a big territory."

Bunion uttered a grunt. "John must have hit you harder than I thought. You don't have a clue as to what's going on."

"It really isn't any of my business. My job is only to deliver goods."

"Well, you seen the law in these parts. Cole ain't going to step in and stop any major fight. He about got whupped one night when a painted lady and one of the farmer gals got into it. Had either of them had the mind, they could have made old Jack look about as sorry as his cat."

"Well, it's like I tried to tell John Fairbourn, I'm not the one who made the wire, and I don't sell it either. My job was to deliver the freight, that's all." He looked around and found his gun and belt at the foot of the bed. Stiffly, laboriously, he rose slowly up onto his feet and strapped it on.

"When do you think Cline will come in?"

"Right sudden, I imagine. Cole said that Dexter's brother put up some of the money for the wire. I reckon Dexter and the other farmers also pooled every cent they had between them for its delivery."

"How do you know so much about it?"

"Cole is the telegrapher."

"Sending a telegraph message is supposed to be private."

Bunion shrugged. "Cole and I are friends, have been for fifteen years. He trusts me."

Luke removed his timepiece. It was a few minutes past noon. "Where can we get something to eat?"

"We?"

"You sent for Cline and put me up here. I owe you at least the price of a meal."

"I was going to add the charges to tending those mules of yours, but I'll take the meal too."

"Whatever."

"The Ace High Saloon is the only eating place in town. Not too bad when the Chinaman is there."

"They've got a Chinese cook?"

"Lee Chan makes some real fine dishes, plus he can cook a steak in such a way that it melts in your mouth."

"What do you usually have?"

"Number three."

Luke threw him a sharp glance. "Number three?"

"Most in town can't remember the names of those Chinese dishes, so he sells them by number. One has some rice and stuff, Two has an egg muffin covered with gravy, and Three has all kinds of vegetables diced up in a sort of stringy stew."

"Now that you've explained it to me, it makes the choice much easier. I was afraid I wouldn't know what I was ordering."

"That's me, sonny, always willing to lend a hand."

Chapter Eight

Unable to chew decently, Luke let Chan fix him something called egg flower soup and then had a bowl of steamed rice. His stomach did some major complaining as Bunion wolfed down a sizzling steak that looked and smelled delicious.

"What now?" Bunion asked as they left the Ace High Saloon.

"I think I'll lie down for a few minutes. I've got more body aches than a pigpen has flies."

"Oops!" Bunion reached out with a hand and caught hold of his arm. He glanced at him, but the liveryman nodded across the street. "Looks as if someone come to visit you."

Timony stopped in her tracks, obviously spying the two of them at the same time. She was wearing a buckskin jacket, a split riding skirt, boots, and the same hat as when driving her wagon from Rimrock. She hesitated, then appeared to firm her resolve, and walked toward them.

"Looks like a one-man job coming thisaway,"

Bunion observed. "I'll mosey off and make myself scarce for a bit."

Rather than forcing Timony to make her way to him, Luke started in her direction and met her halfway. She timidly approached until she was to within a step of him. When she stopped, her sloe eyes lifted to appraise the discolored marks and swelling about his face. With a hint of lightness to her voice, she offered, "You look better than I expected."

It hurt to smile, but Luke suffered the discomfort. "And you're a might prettier than I remembered."

A pink hue glowed about her cheeks. "I…I'm sorry, Mr. Mallory. I didn't know my brother was waiting in town to beat you senseless."

"I consider myself a fair hand in a fight, but he sure enough boxed my ears."

"I…"She lowered her head, apparently unable to find the words she wanted. "Gracious!" she declared, "I hate this!"

"What?"

"Apologizing!" She flashed her dark eyes at him again.

"Especially when it's your own fault!"

"My fault?"

"You're the one who brought a load of that filthy, stinking barbed wire to Broken Spoke! It shouldn't be on my head that John beat you like a dirty rug!"

"I don't recall blaming you."

"Stop it!" She fumed. "Don't you dare be big-hearted and forgiving about this! I feel…I…" She again was at a loss for words. She stomped her foot into the dust in frustration. "Curse your rotten hide, Luke Mallory!" she blurted out at last. "I've said I'm sorry! That's why I came to town!"

"Chan has some fine-tasting lemonade at the saloon," Luke volunteered. "How about I fetch you a glass, and we can sit in the shade and visit a spell?"

"I don't want any lemonade."

"Then how about we sit down and talk?"

"No! I told you, I came to say I'm sorry for my brother whaling on you. I've done that."

"Yes, ma'am."

"I've nothing more to say to you."

"Not even good-bye?"

Timony simmered at once. "You're leaving?"

"Soon as I deliver my freight."

"That's fine." She lifted her chin once more. "But I don't have to say good-bye—more like good riddance!"

Luke again managed a painful smile. "You're a right special picture when you get riled."

For an instant, the anger was replaced by a complexed awe on Timony's face. She masked the feeling quickly and gave her head a shake. "You're about as hopeless as a three-legged race horse, Luke Mallory. Someone really ought to lock you away with the other crazy people in the world."

"Yes, ma'am."

Timony whirled about and strode smartly back to where she had tied her horse. Luke watched her go, wondering if he wouldn't be wise to stick around Broken Spoke for a few days. The problem was, there was a job waiting for him, the appointment of a lifetime. Sherman would be expecting his return, ready to show him the ropes of his new job. His agency appointment would make him someone, respected and admired. Never again would he be referred to as "the kid," or considered just another teamster. He would be somebody, a Wells Fargo agent.

"Give her up, Mallory," he muttered under his breath. "Maybe when you have a title and a real job, then you can find a gal like her."

The ranchers all looked to John. He was their leader. Even Henry Fielding, owner of the biggest sheep ranch in the country, waited for John to take the lead.

Sid Renikie grew tired of waiting. "Them sodbusters try fencing off the ponds or streams and I'll be killing me a plowboy."

Fess nodded his head in agreement. "My brother's right. We've got to act before it's too late."

"I agree that we can't let them fence off the water," John agreed, "but there might be a way to compromise."

"Compromise!" Fess cried. "We ran cattle for years, before those clod-kickers came into Broken Spoke Valley and started ripping open the earth, ruining miles and miles of open range. Maybe you've been out in the sun too long, John!"

"I'm not saying we let them cut our range into pieces, Fess."

"You can be bighearted about this," the man retorted. "Those farmers barely made a dent on your grazing. We lost the use of two water holes and a thousand acres by them homesteaders. Now they want to take even more and fence off our access to more water holes!"

"I know you boys got hit the worst, but your ranch had most of the prime farmland in Broken Spoke."

"And we let them take it away," Sid said with a growl. "You can't seriously expect us to take this lying down?"

"Just what are you saying, John?" another rancher asked. "You want us to sit back and let them put in their fences?"

"First off, I want to set up a meeting with Cline and see what the farmers have in mind. It won't do us much harm, if they only use the wire to keep the cattle out of their crops."

"It ain't going to happen that way!" Fess snapped. "My cousin was over in Colorado, when the farmers started fencing with barbed wire. They not only closed off their own land, but cut off the cattle from the free range and most of the water. When the fences were cut, the farmers complained to the governor, and he sent the law to haul the fence cutters off to jail. That devil's rope is intended to end the open range. The farmers won't be happy until every steer is shut into a tiny pen. When that happens, we'll all be flat busted."

There was a round of agreement in the room. Even Fielding bobbed his head up and down. "I must agree with Fess. I've twelve thousand head of woollybacks, and there will be a shearing crew of twenty men coming here next week for harvesting the wool. Now isn't the time for me to be fretting over whether or not I'm going to be able to feed and water my flocks."

"It's worse for us ranchers," Fess continued. "Each and every steer needs no less than ten acres to grow healthy and fat. We start cutting all the corners off of the range and it'll mean selling off part of our herd to survive."

The sound of a horse coming into the yard turned all heads to the yard. Billy was near a window and looked out. "Timony," he said.

A moment later the door opened. Timony was not surprised at the company, having seen all the horses tied off at the corral. She paused long enough to acknowledge each of those present.

"Didn't take long for the Ranchers Association to gather," she said, looking at her older brother. "Do you have a plan?"

"Not yet."

"Well, it doesn't have to include the freighter. He's pulling out, soon as Cline accepts delivery of his wire."

John rubbed the swollen knuckle on one hand. "I knew trying to talk to him was a waste of time."

Billy chuckled. "Talk, he says. Was it a kind of sign language you used, big brother?"

Everyone in the room grinned or laughed, except Timony. She remained stolid, waiting for someone to tell her what had been decided.

"John's feeling benevolent," Fess finally said to

her. "He thinks the farmers might be willing to only fence in their crops." With a negative shake of his head, "only that would mean using two or three times the amount of wire to do the same job as if they simply cut the land into sections."

"He's right," Fielding agreed. "To fence around every plowed field would take longer and use a whole lot more wire than if they run a single stretch of fence between the basin and free range. That would cut off our animals from any farms completely."

"Not to mention half of the watering holes," Sid put in.

"We ain't going to let them do it!" another objected. "If they put up a single strand of wire, we ought to hang them with it!"

There was a round of agreement. Fess pounded his fist into the palm of his hand. "We've always kept wire out, John. I don't see any reason to change our minds this go-round."

"We don't want a bloody war, Fess."

"I ain't going to sit back and let them cut our land up into tiny pieces!"

"I'm only saying that there might be alternatives. It was my father who learned us that we could live with Fielding and his sheep." He threw a hard look around the room at each man. "Who remembers when all of the ranchers were of a mind to run him and his woolly herds out of the territory?"

"This is different," Fielding was the one to speak. "My sheep did nothing to reduce the size of the range or block off the water holes. When they string their barbed wire, it will be the end of grazing in this country."

"Fielding's right!" Sid agreed.

"That's how I see it too," Fess put in. "Even one strand of wire is too much."

"The answer is to drive the farmers out of the territory!" Sid shouted.

John raised his hands to silence the room. "I'm going to ride in and speak to Cole in town, so he knows what is going on. Our first order of business is to talk. There is always time for a fight, but I say we use that as a last result."

"You didn't try that with the teamster," Timony reminded him curtly. "You about beat his brains out for simply hauling the wire, and now you're going soft on the farmers?"

John studied her for a long, awkward moment. "I'm for thinking that you're the one who's going soft—on that Mallory guy!"

Timony bridled at once. "I believe it's perfectly natural for me to wish to repay a man who helped me out of a fix with something besides a beating."

"Maybe you should have offered him a big kiss as his reward?" Billy teased. "Bet he'd think that was worth helping you out of about any fix."

"You shut up!" she fired at Billy.

"Could be that she already done give him that big kiss," Sid joined in. "Might explain why she's so eager to defend him."

"You shut up too!"

But the room was filled with catcalls and joking.

Timony could not fight with them all. In a huff, she marched through the kitchen and went to her room. When she slammed the door, she could still hear the laughter.

She sat down on the edge of her bed and slowly reclined until she was prone. The light filtered through the pink-curtained window, bathing the room in a mellow glow. Even as her anger waned, she suffered from a churning within her stomach. She told herself it was from the possibility of open range war with the farmers, that men might be beaten or even killed on both sides.

Dexter Cline was determined to make a go of his farm. The farmers would follow his lead, especially the ones like Miller Queen and his sons. They had been in a number of fights and constant trouble ever since arriving in Broken Spoke. On the other side, John was the only one who controlled the hotheads like Fess and Sid Renikie. If those two had their way, there would have been a bloody war long ago.

Closing her tired eyes relieved the burning sensation. Timony wondered what was the matter with her lately. Since meeting up with Luke Mallory, she had not been able to sleep. The man inhabited her thinking, invaded her every waking moment. Lately, her stomach seemed to be tied in knots and her chest was filled with a vast, empty feeling.

"Get a grip on the saddle horn, Timony," she told herself firmly. "You are not seated on a dream pony, but are riding a nightmare. Stop letting that man get into your head. I mean it!"

Chapter Nine

Luke had met men like Dexter Cline before, willful and direct. The man was lean and hard in both build and manner, an inch or two taller than Luke and tough as parched leather. He was inflexible, his mind set, with no doubt that he was right in what he was doing. Five other men arrived with him, each with a wagon to haul the wire. Luke usually helped unload his freight, but Cline quickly took command of the situation. He directed the others to start dividing up the wire, while he presented Luke with a bank draft for the wire and shipping charges.

The draft looked good. It was on a merchant's bank in Denver.

"Are you staying in town a few days?" Cline asked as Luke tucked away the piece of paper.

"I've got a new job waiting for me, soon as I get back to Cheyenne. I reckon the team will be rested enough that I can leave tomorrow."

"Looks as if someone gave you a shiner."

"No one gave it to me," Luke joked, "I had to fight for it."

There was a spark of admiration in Cline's flinty expression. "We owe you a debt of thanks for bringing in the wire. You probably knew ahead of time that it would not be a popular idea."

"I had a few misgivings to start with. Subsequently they all proved true."

Cline took his hand in a quick shake. "Well, I wish you luck. Been good doing business with you."

"You too."

Luke watched Cline stride over to where the men were loading wire. He had to revere the courage of the handful of farmers. They had to battle the ranchers, hostile land, and nature's own resentment to forge homes in that part of Wyoming. Men who had such grit would be tough in a range war. They would fight till the last man.

With a mental shrug, Luke decided it was not his problem. The barbed wire had been signed for and delivered. He didn't have to remind himself that he was not a part of the local feud, nor was he responsible for anything that might happen. If he had not transported the load of wire to Broken Spoke, someone else would have.

"No one blames the postmaster for delivering a letter that contains bad news," he muttered to himself. And this was no different.

Except for Timony Fairbourn.

Luke hated the way thinking of her affected him. He had deceived her from the onset, letting her think he was hauling normal supplies. If she had known about the wire, she would have likely not accepted his help when her wagon broke down.

Recalling the moment when he had been sitting with Timony's head cradled in his arms, he remembered her first lucid instant. There had been a brief moment when she looked up at him, when he saw something warm and wonderful in her eyes. She had gazed up at him in a way that could have melted Satan's heart. It was not passion, not any kind of yearning, but more of a subtle, dreamy contentment, as if she was completely at ease within his arms.

He shook the delightful memory from his head and slowly wandered over to a shady spot, where he could watch the remainder of the loading. He would stand by until the count was complete, then he would see that Bunion gave a double portion of oats to his mules. After an inspection of the shoes of each animal and a final night to rest, he would be ready to leave Broken Spoke behind.

Oddly enough, there was some unrest at the thought. He sorely wished he could see Timony again. There was something very special about her, something he would not soon forget.

It was dark, except for the lights coming from the windows of the saloon and a couple buildings along the main street. Bunion allowed him to use the bed for another night, so Luke had taken a nap after finishing with his mules. It took the edge off of his need for sleep, so, after spending an hour listening to

Bunion's endless chatter, he decided to go over to the saloon and see if he could sit in at a card game.

He was on the street, when a shadowy figure stepped out of Jack Cole's office. Luke recognized the frame of John Fairbourn and wondered if he was in town alone, or whether Timony had come with him. He turned in a direction to intercept the man before he could reach his horse.

A muzzle flash came from between two buildings.

The gun blast shattered the stillness of the night. As John sagged to the ground, Luke jerked his own gun free. He fired at the darkness, aiming only at where the muzzle flash had been.

Feeling certain he had missed, Luke started off in the direction of the ambusher. He only managed a few steps before an icy voice stopped him in his tracks.

"Hold it! I've got you in my sights, bushwhacker!"

"He's getting away!" Luke shouted. "The shot came from across the street!"

Men scurried out of the saloon, asking questions, searching the darkness for clues as to what had happened. Cole had come out from his office and was kneeling at John's side.

"Let the gun fall, freighter," the man growled at Luke. "I can't miss from this close."

Luke had no choice. He dropped the Colt onto the ground.

"You get him, Sid?" One of the men from the saloon joined the guy holding Luke under his gun.

"Red-handed, Big George. I seen him fire his gun."

"You saw me shoot at the guy who shot John Fairbourn! You're letting the shooter get away!"

The man called Big George picked up Luke's pistol. "It's warm. Been fired all right."

"I told you…"

"Let's go," Sid ordered. "Cole has a nice warm cell for you for the night. If John don't make it, you'll be swinging at the end of a rope at first light!"

Rather than waste his breath on the two men, Luke walked over to where the men had gathered about John's body.

"Get Bunion over here," Cole ordered no one in particular. "John is hit bad."

"Here's the guy who shot him," Sid told the crowd.

"Get a rope!" someone shouted.

"Hang the no good back-shooter!" another cried.

But Cole rose up onto his feet. "We ain't going to have no lynching in Broken Spoke," he declared.

"The guy who shot John was on the other side of the street," Luke again tried to explain. "I saw the flash from his gun muzzle and fired at him!"

"I was right on top of the whole thing," Sid said, quickly discounting Luke's story. "All I seen was this guy shooting at John."

Bunion came running up the street. He carried a black bag in one hand and was puffing like a wind-broke horse.

"Someone shot?" he gasped.

"John Fairbourn," Cole replied. "Looks pretty bad."

Bunion quickly dropped down beside the body and

found where the bullet had struck him. "A couple inches above the brisket," he announced. "Don't look good."

"Will he make it?" Sid wanted to know.

"Can't tell yet," Bunion said, looking up. He frowned, seeing that Sid was holding a gun on Luke. "Why are you pointing that rabbit killer at Mallory?"

"He done fired the shot that brought down John."

"I shot at the one who ambushed him," Luke said in his own defense. "This guy didn't see anything but my return fire."

"How about John?" Cole asked.

"Let's get him to a bed," Bunion replied. "It looks as if the bullet went right through him. He's got a chance, if it didn't hit anything vital."

Luke was pushed roughly into Cole's office. At the back of the small building was a single cell, a small cubicle, solidly constructed of steel bars and thick cedar slabs. The only furnishings were a cot and a water bucket.

"If I had my way, we'd hang you right now," Sid hissed vehemently.

Luke gave him a sharp look. "That would save a lot of trouble—such as looking for the real shooter!"

With a slam, he closed and locked the steel gate. Then he said: "Save your story for the trial, freighter man. I ain't buying it."

Luke stood back, hands on his hips, and watched the man leave the room. Sid looked to be a cattleman. As such, he was bound to be one of John Fairbourn's supporters. He counted himself fortunate that the man hadn't shot him in the back.

Still, fear set in, an uncertainty that he would survive this. He was innocent, but that didn't matter to anyone at the moment. Logically, there was no reason for Luke to ambush John, unless a judge and jury suspected he was vengeful over being beaten in their fist fight.

With a grim resolve, and able to do nothing but wait, Luke took a moment to brush the cat hair from the blanket and sat down on the bunk. Listening to the sounds from the street, he silently offered up a prayer that John did not die.

Timony was at Bunion's house, seated next to the bed. She stared at her fitfully resting brother. She had never thought of John as vulnerable. He had always been a strong leader, as dependable as the sun. To see him lying unconscious, fighting for his very life, it evoked tears that would not stop.

"He'll make it, Sis," Billy said, standing next to her. "Bunion says the bullet hit him below his collarbone and went out the back of his shoulder. It don't seem to have hit anything vital."

"Bunion's experience as a doctor is limited to his experience as a medic during the war between the Union and Confederacy, Billy. He might be able to prick a boil or stitch up a small cut, but…" She could not finish.

"He's seen a heap of bullet wounds, and I'm sure he's right about the vitals," Billy insisted. "I've hunted many a deer and followed the trail of a hit animal. If the bullet had hit the lung, there would have been foam in the blood. It was a clean wound. I'm telling you, John is going to pull through."

"More than can be said for the freighter." A new voice entered the room.

Timony turned her attention on Fess Renikie. Several years older than John, he had a husky build, a chaw of tobacco tucked into one cheek, and nervous, pale green eyes. He was dressed in range garb, Levi pants, a gray cotton shirt, polished boots, and dress spurs. He held his 'Boss of the Plains' ten-gallon hat in his hands.

"The teamster didn't shoot John," Timony said. "What reason would he have had?"

"Your brother used him as a broom to sweep up the street, Timmy. I reckon he's the kind of man who don't take defeat lightly."

She gave her head a firm shake. "I know him better than you do, Fess. Mr. Mallory was not holding a grudge against John. I spoke to him after their fight. He was going to leave town; he was not looking to get even."

"Sid seen him do it."

"I don't care what Sid thinks he saw. Mr. Cole said he heard two shots. Everyone heard two shots."

"So?"

"If Mr. Mallory fired twice, how come John was only hit once?"

"The man is in cahoots with the farmers. He done brung in the wire!"

"He hauls freight for Wells Fargo. It was his job to deliver the wire. He has no reason to be involved in our petty war."

"You sure seem to think a heap of the freighter."

"I don't want some scapegoat to hang for shooting John. I want the man responsible, Fess."

"A good many people are talking a lynching. How you going to convince them that the freighter didn't do it?"

"I've already asked Mr. Devine to have a hearing."

"A hearing?"

"I've spent a number of evenings talking to a retired judge, who lives at a boardinghouse in Rimrock. We can have what's called a preliminary hearing, to see if there's enough evidence to send for a territorial judge to come up here and hold trial."

"And who presides over something like that?"

"Mr. Devine is the mayor. He can do that much."

"Cartwell Devine owns the Ace High Saloon and holds Sunday meetings. What kind of qualifications are those for sitting in judgment on a case like this?"

"He knows men, and he is the mayor."

Fess frowned. "What if he finds the freighter clear of any charges?"

"Then there is no trial and we know to look for the man who actually shot my brother."

"It ain't going to happen. I tell you, Sid seen Mallory shoot John. He caught him right in the act."

Timony left her brother's side. "We need to speak privately, Fess," she said quietly.

Fess's eyes lit up. "Why, sure, Timmy, anything you say."

Leading the way out of the room, Timony stopped in the hall. When Fess followed after her, she turned to meet him squarely. Fess could sway the ranchers either way. If not for John, he would have been in charge of the Ranchers Association. Impulsive, hostile toward the farmers, he would have had a shooting war ages ago, were it not for her brother. He waited patiently, a gleam twinkling within his eyes.

Except for the yellow teeth and strong breath from chewing tobacco, there was no individual characteristic about Fess that she despised; it was a simple matter of not finding him to her liking. Whenever he looked at her, she felt a trace of apathy, a complete lack of interest. She had no inclination to want to know him better.

"I need you to help me on this, Fess," she murmured. "I'm certain that Mallory did not shoot John."

"What about the evidence?"

"Cole said that Luke claimed he fired at the man who shot John. I believe that's what Sid saw." With a deep breath, she looked Fess squarely in the eyes. "I'm asking that you help keep the ranchers from doing anything rash. John certainly wouldn't want an innocent man hanged or sent to prison."

"I don't get it, Timmy. How can you be so sure the guy ain't guilty?"

"I'm sure," she stated firmly, hating the way he called her by a name she detested. "And I need your help to keep the others sober and prevent them doing something rash."

Fess took a step closer. "You ask a lot, but you don't never give anything in return."

She felt a dark warning cloud cover her. "I don't know what you mean."

"Sure you do," Fess maintained. "For the past year, I've been trying to get you to take a ride with me, go on a picnic, even attend one of the monthly barn dances with me. All I ever got was a tired jaw from talking."

"It isn't you, Fess," she said quickly. "I haven't done those things with anyone else either. I'm not ready for courtship."

"You're not a kid anymore, Timmy. You ought to be looking for a husband, thinking about starting up your own family."

"Age has nothing to do with it. I have to take care of my brothers and help run our ranch. I haven't really had time for being courted."

Fess appeared to do some thinking. "If I stand up for the freighter and get the other ranchers to go along with the ruling by Devine, what then?"

"What do you mean?"

"I mean"—he reached out and took hold of her arms—"what then?" His eyes bore into her. "I only have to say the word and that teamster will hang."

"He's innocent."

"So you say."

"John is my own brother! Don't you think I want the man who shot him to pay for it?"

"All I'm saying is, you'll owe me a big favor. If I keep the noose from going around Mallory's neck, what do I get out of it?"

Timony's heart pumped sluggishly to a stop. "What do you want?"

"You know what I want, Timmy. Allow me to come courting."

The dreaded words carried the weight of doom. "I…" she faltered.

"You got to know, a few words, a drink or two, and the ranchers will take the law into their own hands." He gave a toss of his unkempt hair. "Without my help, the teamster won't ever get himself one of those hearings."

"All right, Fess. You keep the peace, and you may call on me."

Fess was triumphant. "I knew you'd see my side of it, Timmy!" A wide smile curled his slim lips to reveal his rather crooked rows of teeth. "I'll keep the boys in check, and you can have your deal in court tomorrow morning! If Devine rules that the freighter done the shooting, he'll get his trial and be sent to prison. If Devine rules in his favor, we'll let him take his mules and light out of town."

"Thank you, Fess," Timony said softly, consumed with an ominous repulsion over the prospect of being forced into a courtship.

Fess simpered smoothly, "You won't regret this, Timmy. We were meant to be together. You just wait and see."

Timony watched the man spin about and practically

mince away. Once invited, he was going to be hard to ward off. She feared that she had just made a bargain with the devil.

"Wonder if the general store has any garlic?" she muttered under her breath. Then she sighed resignedly and added, "As if bad breath would keep him away!"

Chapter Ten

Dory Queen, Miller's oldest boy, stood at the doorway to Cline's home. He informed him of the events and quickly returned to his horse. As he rode out of the yard, Dexter was aware of his wife moving up behind him.

"Did I hear that John Fairbourn was shot?"

"He ain't dead yet, but he was hit pretty hard. They grabbed the Wells Fargo teamster for it," he said. "Man didn't strike me as the sort who would shoot down someone from ambush."

"You don't think he did it?"

"I don't know any more about it than that, Helen. Dory says they are going to have some kind of hearing to determine if there will be a trial for him or not."

"A preliminary hearing?"

He turned around, surprised at the term. "What do you know about such things?"

She showed a sheepish smile. "I read a couple of those penny dreadfuls Leta buys. You know how she loves to read about gunfighters and such."

"Ain't no such thing as a gunfighter," he said.

"Nothing but wild tales and made-up stories, same as the yarns told to tots at bedtime."

"Yes, dear, I know."

"That gal is going to have us both suffering burning stomachs from her fanciful ways of thinking. If she don't end up married to Billy Fairbourn, she's liable to run off with the first cowboy that comes along with a pearl-handed pistol and a decorated saddle."

"She's eighteen, dear. She has a mind of her own."

Cline narrowed his gaze at Helen. She was a slightly roundish woman, with gray streaks in her hair and the maternal face of a saint. She was as steady as a rock foundation, quick to smile, never seemed to lose her temper, and had the uncanny ability to always see both sides of an issue.

"You know I had to order the barbed wire?"

"Yes, dear."

He loved the way she always called him dear, but he worried what some of the other farmers would think, should they ever overhear the term. He silently vowed to skin alive the first man who made fun of the pet name.

"What do you think, Helen?"

"I think you should arrange to speak to Billy Fairbourn. With John laid up or possibly worse, you need to let the ranchers know what you are planning to do."

"They are sure to try and stop us."

"Oh, I don't think so, not if you explain to them that you only intend to fence off the crops. They know their wandering cattle have ruined a good many of our fields."

"Miller wants to run a fence strip from one end of the valley to the other. He says we can save weeks of work by putting up one single fence to protect all of the farms."

"And how many water holes and stretches of open range would a fence like that cost the ranchers?"

"You siding with them?"

Helen showed her patient smile. "I am concerned for the welfare of my husband and children. Doing what Miller says would cause trouble, and a range war would endanger us all."

"What if they won't listen? What if they start cutting down every fence we put up? We have to protect our crops!"

"Violence should be a last resort, dear, that's all I'm saying."

"Speaking of violence," Dexter said, thinking aloud, "if they don't find that the freighter shot John, you know who they're going to point a finger at next—us!"

Helen frowned at the idea. "Do you think one of the Queen boys would do something like that?"

"I ain't sure. They're pretty wild at times, but I don't know if one of them would try to kill John Fairbourn. When you think on it, John was about as fair-minded as any of the ranchers. He was the one guy I thought we could reason with."

Helen stepped close, slipped her arms around Dexter, and leaned her head against his shoulder. Privacy was not something they had a lot of, with six of them living under the one roof, within the confines of only two rooms. The girls were busy sewing on a group quilt for their bed, while Jimmy was camped on the floor, next to the fireplace, reading a book. None of them seemed to take notice of Dexter and Helen at the doorway, but Dexter nevertheless felt a heat rise to his face.

"It'll be okay," he said gruffly, unable to soften his gravelly voice.

"I trust you'll make it so," Helen murmured. "We have so much to be thankful for, but I…I can't help worrying about this wire thing."

Dexter uttered another sigh. "First chance I get, I'll speak to Billy. It'll take four times as many posts and spools of wire, but we'll only fence off the crops."

Helen did not speak, but squeezed him tightly in her arms. He knew she was manipulating him, using her womanly charms and instinctive sense to direct his actions. However, he could not complain, enjoying the feel of her standing so close. A man had to keep his woman content.

The house was dark and strangely cold. It was as if John's absence had removed the life right from the building. Timony paused in front of the large wood cookstove. She didn't feel like preparing a meal for one. There were a jar with jerky and a basket of hard rolls, so these and a cup of warm cider completed her evening meal.

Once into bed, she was assailed by the quietude and emptiness. It was ridiculously childlike, but she reached out and drew her doll into bed. She held it close, using it as a crutch against the lonely sadness of the house.

Suddenly, there was the sound of someone moving in the next room. Timony sat upright, her heart surging up into her throat. She held her breath, an irrational fear rushing through her. The door opened—

"Timony?" It was Token's wife. "Are you awake?"

"Yes, Linda."

The woman had a candle in her hand. She drew it into the room and held it high so that she could see. Timony hurriedly tucked the doll under the covers, so Linda would not see her acting like a small child.

"Are you all right?"

"Yes."

Linda was a petite woman with silvery hair that was always in a tight bun at the back of her head. She had never seemed a maternal sort, so Timony had always thought it was fortunate that she and Token were childless.

"Token said there was no smoke from your chimney. I brought you over some leftover stew and a piece of corn bread."

"That's very thoughtful of you, Linda. I didn't feel like cooking tonight."

"How is John?"

"Better than we have a right to expect. I'm sure the bullet would have killed a lesser man."

"Was it the teamster? Did he shoot John?"

"No. He claims that he took a shot at the man who

did the shooting. I'm afraid it was too dark and he missed."

"Is there anything you need?"

"No, thank you."

Linda hesitated, as if uncomfortable. "There's something that I wish to say, something I have wanted to say for a long time."

"What is it, Linda?"

"I…I know you have missed your mother all these years, Timony." Linda's voice was a mere whisper. "I often listened to you cry yourself to sleep at nights, after she was taken from us." The woman paused, as if unable to find the right words.

"I remember that you and she were quite close," Timony offered, "more like sisters than two people working on the same ranch."

"Yes, she was very special to me, the only real friend I ever had." Linda wrung her hands. "I was always an awkward child, a loner, thin and homely."

"I've never thought of you as being plain or homely, Linda."

She smiled, something Timony had rarely seen her do. "You are a sweet child, Timony. I wish…" She took a deep breath. "I wish I could have comforted you, those many nights. It isn't that I didn't wish to, it's only…I mean…"

"I know what you mean, Linda," Timony said softly, "really, I do."

A wave of relief passed over Linda's face, as if she had finally confessed something dreadful. "I put the stew and corn bread on the table."

"Thank you, again. That was very thoughtful of you."

"Good night, Timony."

"Good night, Linda."

Then the woman withdrew from the room. Timony listened to her go out the back and close the door. She had never thought of Linda as being compassionate, due to the fact she was a quiet woman who never displayed much emotion. It was strange to discover that her actions, or lack of attention, were because she was shy and uncertain.

Viewing her in such a light, she considered Luke Mallory. He had a confidence about him, yet there was an underlying ambiguity in his character. It was as if he thought of himself as a man, fully capable of doing whatever job was put before him, yet he had a doubting side. He was lacking something in his life. Either that, or he wanted something so desperately, it haunted his every waking moment.

Is it a woman he needs? Timony wondered. *Or is it something else, perhaps a goal he feels he has to accomplish?*

The saloon was filled to capacity, with a good many people crowded into the doorway or listening from the street. The hearing was informal, with Cartwell Devine presiding like a judge. He wore no black robe, but had combed his hair and shaved for the occasion. For his podium, he had placed a desk on the crudely built platform, which had been constructed to accommodate the traveling parson, who came by two Sundays a month to preach the Gospel. He pounded the butt of his pistol on the desktop.

"Settle down, folks! let's have some quiet in the court." The room fell silent almost at once. "That's better," he said importantly. "We are not here as a kangaroo court or public tribunal. This here is a hearing, so called, as it is to decide if we have reason to wire the circuit judge to head this way for a real trial. As such, there ain't no jackleg lawyers either representing the accused or pointing fingers. There is only me. I'll ask the involved parties to speak and that's it."

He paused to make eye contact with Luke. "Being that you're the one with the most to lose or gain from this hearing, Mr. Mallory, I grant you the right to ask questions of anyone who gives testimony. Fair enough?"

"Yes, sir," Luke answered. "I appreciate that."

Cartwell puffed up his chest a trifle, filled with a confidence that he was doing a good job.

"Sid Renikie, as you brung Mallory in at gunpoint, you can give us your account first. Stick to what you done seen with your own eyes. Don't get off to speculating the whys or wherefors."

"Sure, Cart."

"Stand up and give your deposition."

"My what?"

"Tell us what you seen."

"Oh!" Sid stood up. "Let's see, I was just coming out of the Ace High—been playing over at the corner table with Big George and a couple other fellas. It was mostly penny ante, but I won a couple dollars and some change."

"Stick to the shooting, Sid," Cartwell said. "Ain't no one interested in your run of luck at the card table."

Sid furrowed his brow like a scolded child. "Okay, Cart, okay. What I seen was this joker here shooting at John Fairbourn."

"Be specific."

"What?"

"Tell us every detail of what you seen going on."

Sid pondered in silence for a few seconds. "I heard the shooting about the time I walked out. Then I seen the teamster fire at John. I drawed down on him and made him drop his gun."

"May I?" Luke asked.

"You're entitled," Cartwell answered back.

"How many shots did you see me fire, Sid?"

"Jus' once," he replied. "I didn't see you fire the first shot."

"That's my only question, Mr. Devine."

Cartwell nodded, told Sid to sit down, and turned to Jack Cole. "How about you, Jack? What did you see?"

"I didn't see the shooting at all," he admitted, "but I sure enough heard two shots. They was maybe a second or two apart." A dozen men in the room bobbed their heads up and down in agreement. All of them had heard two gunshots. "John and I had just finished talking and he went out of my office. The door barely closed when I heard the first shot. Before

I could get up and hobble outside, there was a second shot fired. John was already lying on the ground when I spotted his body."

Cartwell looked around the room. "Did anyone else see the shooting?" When no one answered, he turned back to Jack. "Anything you want to add?"

"Well, I don't believe Mallory done the shooting, if that makes a difference."

"We don't entertain opinions, Jack."

"Marshal Cole?" Luke spoke up. "After my gun was given to you, did you inspect it?"

"I did."

"How many empty chambers did you find?"

"There was one spent cartridge."

"And you are certain that you heard two shots?"

"Definitely."

"How do you account for only one bullet being fired from my gun, if I was the one who shot John?"

"Like I said, I never figured you done it to start with."

"That will do, Jack," Cartwell told him. "You have said your piece."

Cole sat down, and Cartwell looked over at Bunion. "You told me before we began that you had something to add to this hearing, Mr. Jones."

"That's right."

"So, let's hear it."

"I ain't no detective, but I've treated many a gunshot wound in my day," Bunion began. "When you look at the facts, I'm inclined to agree with Cole that Mallory was not the one who did the shooting."

"Explain yourself, Bun ... eh, Mr. Jones."

"Well, John come out the front door of Cole's place. That would put him facing the street. He was shot below the collarbone here." He pointed to a spot a couple inches to the left of his wishbone. "The exit wound was here." He put his right hand on his shoulder and showed the mayor. "From the angle of his injury, it is obvious that whoever done the shooting was off to his right side." He tipped his head toward Luke. "Sid was there to grab Mallory, but they were both to John's left. No way he could have shot John at such an angle from that side."

There was a lot of whispering back and forth in the room. Cartwell studied the information for a moment, then cleared his throat. When that was not enough to quiet the crowd, he hammered on his desk with the butt of his gun.

"Shut up, in the gall-durned courtroom!" he snapped. "What do you people think this is, a horse auction?"

Silence fell over the crowd.

"That's better," Cartwell declared. "I'm ready to make my decision on this case, so listen up!" He swept the room with his dark gaze. No one uttered a sound, and a few were holding their breath.

"It is clear to me that there's been a miscarriage of justice here. Mallory's gun was only fired once, and Bunion has explained how the shot had to have come from the opposite side from where Mallory was standing. It don't take a genius to figure that Sid done grabbed the wrong man."

"I agree," Cole spoke up.

"No one asked you," Cartwell grumbled. "The decision is mine to make."

"Sorry, Cart."

Cartwell lifted his chin and swept over the room with a confident gaze. He spoke in a resounding, clear voice. "While I am not an actual magistrate for the court, I am required to make a determination of our findings. I therefore do not find any evidence against Mr. Mallory which would hold up in a court of law. It is the order of this hearing that it was some other person who fired the shot that injured John Fairbourn." He turned his gaze toward Luke. "You are a free man, Mr. Mallory."

Bunion let out a cheer, but cut it abruptly short, when he realized that he was the only one outwardly applauding the decision. He awkwardly cleared his throat as a number of people looked in his direction.

Luke had been worried all morning. Being innocent would not have helped, if Bunion and Cole had not stood up for him. It had also been in his favor that Cartwell was an honest man. As the old marshal returned his gun and belt to him, he was finally able to breathe normally again.

"Sorry for the inconvenience, sonny," he said, working up a haggard smile. "Leastwise you are cleared."

"No real harm done," Luke replied as he strapped on his Colt, "other than the fact that we let the real shooter get away."

"There wasn't a moon out when John was shot.

Even if you had given chase, it would have been real tough to catch the bushwhacker in the dark."

"Did you do some looking around?"

"I walked the area you indicated, but there was no shell casing or any readable prints. Probably a dozen people walked over betwixt those two buildings after the shooting."

"I doubt that there would have been any spent shell. The sound of the gun was that of a pistol, probably a .44 or .45 caliber."

"That narrows it down some," Cole said and grunted. "Ain't more'n half the men in the valley what carries one of them on his hip."

A couple townsmen came by to shake Luke's hand or congratulate him on being innocent. He accepted the tidings with humility and glanced about the throng of people. He had hoped that Timony would come speak to him, but she and her brother had already left the room.

"How was John this morning?" he asked, after most had cleared the room.

"Better. Bunion says Timony and Billy are going to bring in a wagon and take him home in a day or two. There's a good chance that he'll be up and about in a couple weeks."

"That's good news."

Cole removed a piece of paper from his pocket and unfolded it. "By the way, sonny, I got some other information on you while I was sending out wires."

"Why bother?"

"I wanted to know if you was guilty or not." He

showed a snaggletooth grin. "Always prefer to know something about a man I might have to hang."

"Thoughtful of you."

"I sent a wire to that company, Washburn & Moen. They put me onto the Wells Fargo and American Express people in Cheyenne for information about you. Seems they think very highly of you."

"I've worked for them for the past five years."

"And you have a job waiting for you as an agent for one of their offices. That's a real show of confidence."

"Only after I agreed to deliver the wire to Broken Spoke."

"I also found out that you were once a deputy sheriff in Abilene under Wild Bill Hickok!"

"We never called him Wild Bill, and our title was policemen, but I only had the job for a few months. It was no big deal."

"I heard about Hickok being killed a couple years back, shot in the back by some coward."

"Only way anyone would dare take on Hickok was from the back."

"So?"

"So what?"

"I'm looking for some help here, sonny. I'd admire for you to pin on a badge and help me for a short spell."

Luke eyed Cole as if his pants had just caught fire and he didn't have the brains to run for water. "That there is a twisted sense of humor you're sportin', pops. One minute, you're about to put a noose around my neck, and now you want to hire me on as your deputy?"

"Only till we find out who shot John Fairbourn, and the problem is settled over the barbed wire."

"Do I have an 'I'm stupid' sign painted on my back? There ain't a reason in the world for me to get involved in the battle between the ranchers and the farmers here in Broken Spoke."

"None?"

"None!"

Cole gave a tip of his head toward the window. Two riders were leaving town, Billy and Timony Fairbourn.

"I can think of at least one reason."

Luke attempted to mask his feelings. "There's nothing between us."

"She stood up for you, sonny. It was her big brother who was shot, yet she came by to tell me you were innocent."

"I am innocent."

"Worse than that," Cole continued his argument, "Billy told me that, on your behalf, she had to consent to let Fess Renikie come courting."

"What do you mean, my behalf?"

"Billy overheard her talking to Fess—it was his brother, Sid, who brung you in. Anyway, he was threatening to get a mob riled and hang you last night. The only way she could stop him was to agree to let him come courting. You owe her for that."

"Maybe she wants him to come courting," Luke said, hating the way his stomach began to churn at the thought. "She probably likes the guy."

"Sure enough," Cole said, "about as much as having a scorpion in her drawers."

"This isn't my fight!"

"Bunion said you and Timony were a good match for a double harness. That gal needs a good man, and both he and I think you're the fellow what fits the wagon."

He stared at the old man. "I can't imagine why you're not married, Cole. You've got such a wonderful way with words concerning romance."

"So I'm as tactless as a pig in a wallow. What can I say, women never fancied me none."

"I've got a good job waiting for me, and it will be a whole lot less dangerous than what you are offering."

Cole squinted at him under bushy brows, his bright eyes probing for any give in Luke's makeup. "You won't never find another gal like Timony, sonny," he continued. "Let her slip away and you'll hate yourself for the rest of your life."

Luke stared off in the direction Timony had ridden, He couldn't leave without seeing her first, but he wasn't ready to mix himself into the valley feud. "I'll give it some thought, Cole, but I have a job waiting for me. Come tomorrow, I'll likely take my mules and head out."

Chapter Eleven

The three riders caught the Clines by surprise. "Take a squint at that, Tito," Fess said with a growl, sitting like a king atop his horse, "the Clines are stringing wire to keep out the cattle."

"Make a good many sheep unhappy also," Tito agreed, sitting a nervous mount at his side. "I think we best go and warn the others. We soon won't have the water or feed for our animals."

Johnny carefully and deliberately put down his hammer. He tossed a hasty look over his shoulder for help. Dexter, however, had gone to the house to sharpen the shovels. Leta removed her pair of thick gloves and quickly slipped between her brother and the three men on horseback.

"We're only fencing in the cornfield," she explained. "It won't hurt your cattle or your sheep."

Sid neck-reined his horse, jumping it forward. The sudden movement drove Leta's two sisters back, right up against the barbed wire. Sally caught her sleeve on a barb and squealed. It brought a cruel snigger from Fess.

"These little heifers don't seem to like the wire," Sid taunted. "How do you gals think our cattle feel?" He jerked the reins of his horse and caused the animal to turn sharply into the two girls. Sally was knocked backward, against the wire. As she fell to the ground, the spiked barbs dug into her tender flesh.

"Stop it!" Leta cried out, pushing with all her might against Sid's horse. She hurried to pull Sally away from the wire. The youngest of the Cline family was crying, and there was a trickle of blood showing from two deep scratches on her shoulder and arm.

"Leave us be!" Johnny charged forward to confront Sid. "We ain't hurting your cattle none."

Fess slid down from his saddle. Before Johnny was aware that one of the men was on the ground, Fess grabbed hold of him and spun him around. A brutal fist smashed the boy in the face. Before he could recover, Fess hammered him twice more and knocked him to the ground.

Johnny rolled over onto his stomach, dazed and bleeding. Fess might have kicked him while he was down, but Leta attacked him from behind.

"You vile creature!" she shrieked, slapping and pounding Fess about the head. He covered up to protect himself, and Sid again used his horse, this time to separate the two of them. He swung the free end of the reins like a belt strap, swatting Leta across the face.

"Back off, you she-devil!" he snarled.

Leta gave ground, throwing up her hands to protect herself. She backed up a few steps, then put a hand up to rub the welt on her cheek. Glowering still, she rasped, "You're such brave men, attacking three girls and a boy."

"I think they've gotten the message," Tito told Fess. "No need picking on a bunch of kids."

Fess was caught up with the fever of dishing out more punishment, but regained control. He gave a last look at Johnny and then mounted his horse. He nodded to his brother. "Tito's right, Sid, but let's take a little something with us."

All three men removed their ropes and shook out loops. Then they all picked out different posts and tossed their loops over the top end. As they rode off, they each dragged away a portion of the fence.

Luke watched for Timony's return. With John bed-ridden, and not yet able to make the trip home, she came into town each evening to bring him his supper. She rode in an hour before dusk and went to the stable to leave her horse. For a change, Bunion was busy, so Luke slipped into the barn. Timony had dismounted and was tying off the horse as he approached.

Not hearing his steps, Timony turned around and jumped from surprise. "Luke Mallory! You about stopped my heart!"

Luke smiled. "I reckon that makes us even then." A hint of rose color crept up into her cheeks. "What are you doing here? I mean, I thought you would be gone by this time."

"I didn't want to leave without seeing you again."

"Seeing me?" Her lids hid her eyes as she appeared

to have a sudden interest in her shoes. "Why should you want to see me again?"

"To thank you, for one thing. There were a good number who wanted to stretch my neck for the shooting of your brother. You sticking up for me probably saved my hide."

"I'm beginning to think it was poor judgment on my part. After bringing in that vicious barbed wire, you deserved to be hanged."

Luke took a step in her direction. It caused Timony's gaze to lift. He perceived a flicker of anticipation within her marine-colored eyes. More than interest, less than alarm.

"I reckon I should have told you from the first that I was hauling wire."

"It would have been more honest than calling that malicious twine farm supplies!"

"I had to bring the load of wire to Broken Spoke," he explained. "It was more than only a freight job, it was a career step, a big one."

"One step from a noose, that's what it was."

"I mean to be someone of importance one day soon, Miss Fairbourn. Governors, senators, bankers, and powerful men from big cities all around will know my name. I'll have dinner with the mayor, maybe end up on the town council. I'll be a known and respected man."

"And that's the only thing of consequence to you, being known and respected?"

Luke hated the way that sounded. ' 'Wells Fargo has

offices all over the country. They are recognized at the country's biggest and best express company."

"You already work for them."

He could see and hear the matter-of-fact influx in her voice. "Yes, but I'll be one of their agents, Miss Fairbourn. I'll be somebody."

"You're somebody now. I don't see what difference a title makes."

Luke hesitated, having never told anyone his true feelings. It was difficult to speak of such things. However, he sincerely wanted Timony to understand his motives, to know and support his desires.

"My parents both died when I was little. At six years of age, I was passed around from neighbor to bum, anyone who would throw me a scrap of food or give me a place to sleep. I wasn't Luke Mallory, I was the runt, the kid, an unwanted alley cat. I got pushed around until I was big enough to fight back, then I ended up as a personal slave for a man who owned a livery stable. I called him uncle, but his only affection for me was for the chores I could handle. It wasn't until I went off to war that anyone ever called me by my right name."

Timony regarded his confession steadily, as if making an appraisal. When she spoke, her voice was cool and aloof.

"My parents are dead too, Mr. Mallory. I suppose I can understand why you feel the way you do." She visibly inhaled deeply. "But it is not a person's place in society that makes them worthwhile. What you are is not nearly so important as who you are. A job position doesn't make you a better person."

"It sure enough means a great deal to some people."

"To some, yes."

"But not you?"

"No."

Luke furrowed his brow. He had thought to impress Timony with news of his upcoming appointment. Instead, she dismissed it as trivial. What was wrong with the girl? Didn't she know what a step like this meant to a man?

"I reckon you ain't fascinated none, being that you aren't interested in me personally. With dozens of suitors, and being pretty as you are, I suppose you have all the choices in the world. I have to make my own future."

She cocked a single eyebrow at him. "Is that your idea of paying me a compliment?"

"What?"

"Tossing out the word *pretty* like it was a six-foot loop and I was a yearling calf?"

"I didn't mean…"

"You didn't mean that you think I'm pretty?"

"You're twisting things around!"

Her eyes were alive with a mischief, but her words were as cool and easy as if they were speaking of the weather. "So you *do* think I'm pretty?"

Luke was taken back by the frankness of the question. He wondered if she was toying with him, but there was no visible scorn, no mockery, no humor.

"I reckon."

"Oh, you reckon, do you?"

"What more do you want?"

"Is that your answer to everything, an *I reckon*?"

Rather than continued along such a ludicrous line, Luke reached out and took hold of Timony's shoulders. He pulled her close and planted his mouth over hers. He was prepared for a struggle, possibly a kick to the shin, perhaps a dig of her nails.

Timony, however, did none of those things. Rather, she shocked him to his boots! She kissed him back!

The cattle were bawling, standing in a bunch, unable to reach their usual watering hole. Cully Deeks rode up to the front of the small herd and jerked his horse to a stop. Swearing vehemently, he reached back into his saddlebags and pulled out a pair of wire cutters. This was something he had feared. No sooner had Big George told him about the arrival of barbed wire in the valley than he knew there would be trouble. He clenched his teeth, furious at the smugness of Miller Queen. The fence prevented the cattle from being able to get to the only water within five miles.

Cully tied off his horse and began to snip the wires and pull them off to one side. Even then, the cattle did not enter without being encouraged. Several had scratches on their noses from having attempted to walk between the posts. Finding it difficult to see the strings of wire, some still seemed to think the wire was in place.

The noise of the cattle covered the sound of approaching riders. By the time Cully realized that Miller and his two boys were approaching, it was too late to mount up and escape. He put his hand on the butt of his gun, glowering at the three men.

"You done crossed the line, Deeks," Miller said, surveying the cut and twisted stands of wire. "I'll be expecting payment for what you've done here."

"Well, I ain't packin' no gold or silver, Queen," Cully drawled. "If'n you want payment, I'll pay you off in lead!"

Dory and Chad edged off to either side. It was impossible for Cully to watch all three men. When Dory reined up and began to dismount, Cully's attention was drawn to his action.

Chad jumped his horse forward and came off in a dive. Before Cully could whirl about to meet his attack, Chad's body slammed into his. The two of them went down in a tangle of arms, legs, and flying fists.

Cully was a game fighter, but Dory pounced on him from behind. He could not beat off both men at the same time. Within seconds, he was winded, bleeding, and overpowered by the two Queen boys.

"Time we showed you cowboys that we farmers are here to stay," Miller announced.

"You squatters will be staying, all right," Cully snarled back, "buried under six feet of sod!"

Miller laughed. "You and the cattle are leaving, Deeks." He began pulling on a pair of heavy leather gloves. "Maybe you'd be good enough to deliver a message to Big George and the other ranchers."

Chapter Twelve

Cole cast a curious look at Luke, as he came back from shaving. "You still here?"

"I don't know how to tell you this, Cole, but I think your mangy cat is in love with me."

He laughed, showing his few rotted stumps for teeth. "I seen that she had taken up sleeping at the foot of your bed, Mallory. Lucky for you, I'm not a jealous man."

"I coughed up a fur ball last night. I'm surprised you are still able to breathe. I never seen so much hair from one critter."

"You're right about that. I'll bet I could stuff a dozen mattresses with the cat hair that's lying about."

Luke let out a deep breath. "Can I get you to send a wire for me?"

"Sure thing, who to?"

"Sherman Porter, head of the Wells Fargo office."

Cole grinned. "You sticking around?"

"I've a mind to see if I can find out who put a slug through John Fairbourn."

"What about the barbed wire?"

"I'll see if I can help with that too, but"—he pointed a finger at Cole—"I don't intend to be stuck here for a month."

"Glad to have you with me, sonny." He opened a desk drawer and removed a badge. "Here you are, all sworn in and legal."

"Any idea who might have shot John?"

"Could have been a farmer, but it don't make a lot of sense."

"How about the other ranchers? Any of them have reason to take out the elder Fairbourn?"

"I don't think so."

"You don't seem to have many suspects, Cole."

"Nary a one."

"All right, I'll do some asking around town. Tomorrow, I'll ride out and meet with the farmers."

"There's no charge for the telegram. I'll explain that you've agreed to help us find an ambusher. Other than that, your room is free, 'less you grab some criminal type and stick him in there. Then you'll have to find another place to stay."

"I understand, Cole. What's the job pay?"

"I just told you."

"I get a bunk in the cell? That's it? Not even my meals?"

He frowned. "I'll see if I can work something out with the Chinaman. I suppose we ought to pay for your keep."

"Very considerate of you."

"You know I can't ride a horse, Mallory. You'll be on your own for most of this."

"I know."

"Bunion can still ride, and he's a passable shot."

"Think he would let me tape his mouth shut, so I didn't have to listen to his tall tales?"

"No, that's the price you pay for his help."

"I'm not sure he'd be worth that much."

"Anything I can do, Mallory, you let me know."

Luke went out of the office. He had packed his things, checked the mules over a last time, even went looking for Bunion to settle his account. Ending up in Cole's office was still something of a surprise. He had been so sure of his goal, to become somebody, to earn his post as an agent for Wells Fargo. Now he had found something—someone!—more important. Timony had come to mean more to him even than becoming an agent. He wasn't quite sure what it meant, but he knew he couldn't leave town until he was sure she would be safe.

Pausing in the morning sun, he looked up and down the street. "I wonder how Bill Hickok would handle an investigation like this?"

Timony and Billy rode into the yard. Dexter came out of the house to greet them, with his Henry rifle in his hands and a sneer on his lips!

"Don't bother to light down, Fairbourn. You two ain't welcome here."

"Mr. Cline," Timony replied, "we need to talk."

Dexter swung his rifle around so the muzzle was pointed between Timony and her brother. "I don't see that we have any talking to do."

"Cully Deeks was beaten and then wrapped in barbed wire and tied to the back of his horse!" Billy said hotly. "What's the matter with you people?"

"Warn't my doing."

Timony leaned toward Dexter, attempting to reach him with her sincerity. "Cully told Big George that you farmers had fenced off the water holes. I thought we were agreed that you were only going to protect your crops."

Dexter's frown was evidence that he had no knowledge of her accusation. He was silent for a few seconds. Before he could reply, Helen Cline stepped out behind her husband.

"Perhaps you should tell them what happened to Sally, dear."

"Sally?" Timony asked. "What about your girl?"

"The Renikie boys were over to visit, along with that Mexican gunman, Tito. The kids were up stringing wire at the head of the corn field. Sid jumped his horse at the girls and knocked Sally into the wire. She has several deep scratches on her arm and back. Then Fess beat up my boy when he tried to stop them. If Tito hadn't called them off, the Renikie brothers might have really done my kids some harm."

"This is crazy!" Timony cried. "We don't want a full-scale war!"

"We didn't start it."

Billy glared at Dexter. "You call bringing wire in and fencing off the water holes not starting it? You knew we would have to fight back!"

"I ain't fenced no water hole, Fairbourn, and yet

the Renikie boys ride over here and start trouble. This here gate swings both ways."

"We'll have a talk with Fess and straighten this out," Timony promised.

Dexter peered hard at her, then slowly relaxed. "You ain't got a whole lot of weight to toss about, without John backing you up. He was the only one who ever tried to keep the ranchers in line."

"He won't be up and around for weeks yet," Timony informed him. "We can't sit back and wait for him to be able to sit a horse. The fighting has got to stop now."

Dexter lowered the rifle. "I keep telling you, our aim is to fence the fields, so the cattle don't eat and stomp the crops to dust. That's the only thing I'm interested in. As far as Miller and the others, I expect each of them is doing what they think is best."

"Even if it starts a war?"

"I ain't never pushed for a fight," Dexter answered. "We don't want no bloody war with none of you."

"What about Miller and his boys?"

"I'll speak to him, but he has a mind of his own."

Neither Timony nor Billy spoke again. They pulled their horses about and rode out of Cline's yard. When they were a quarter-mile distant, Timony turned to her brother.

"We need someone to help us, Billy. Without John, no one is going to take the two of us seriously."

"I think you're right, Sis, but who do we get? Tito is likely the most feared man in the valley, but I wouldn't trust him no more than I would a pet rattlesnake."

"Maybe Fess?"

Billy uttered a cynical snort. "Yeah, and I can guess the price of getting him to help. You ready to marry him?"

"We have to do something to stop this. Big George is going to want revenge for what the Queens did to Cully Deeks. And if Tito is riding with Fess and Sid, they have already begun to initiate a fight."

"So, I'm listening, Sis. Who do you have in mind?" Billy lifted a shoulder in a helpless gesture. "I mean, Jack Cole don't even ride a horse. Besides which, he is too old and stove up to go around threatening anyone."

"There must be someone."

"How about your teamster pal?"

"Mallory?"

"Sure! he's the perfect choice. He is more or less neutral, being as he works for Wells Fargo, and he was a deputy once. He might be able to reason with both sides."

"He has a special job waiting for him. I imagine he's left town by this time."

Billy's brows arched. "A job?"

"A big promotion. He said he was going to be appointed to the position of agent and run an office for Wells Fargo."

"When did you find all this out?"

Timony averted her gaze. "I ran into him last evening, when I was in town."

"He was still in town this morning, when I went in to check on John," Billy pondered aloud. "That's kind of strange, him still hanging around."

Timony felt a lightness enter her being, but smothered it at once. "So he hasn't left yet. What difference does that make?"

"I was only saying it's odd, if he's in such a rush to leave."

"It's his own business when he decides to go!"

"You don't have to get testy."

"I'm not! I told you the man has his own ambitions. He thinks being an agent will make him somebody important."

"I'd have to agree with that," Billy said. "Being an agent for Wells Fargo is a high-class position."

"Do you judge a man by how he acts and what he does, or is it only the job he has?"

"It ought to be what he does."

"Good."

"But there are times when a job makes a difference," he said and grinned. "I'd sure think a Wells Fargo agent was a better choice for a brother-in-law than a high-handed blowhard like Fess Renikie."

"Billy!" Timony snapped, whirling toward him. "I'm going to take a club to you!"

Billy kicked his horse into a run. "Sorry I can't stay and palaver," he called over his shoulder, "but I need to check on Token and see if he needs help at the ranch!"

Timony's horse danced sideways, wanting to bolt forward after Billy. She kept a tight rein, holding the mare back. After a moment, the animal settled down once more, and she was able to concentrate on what should be her next move.

With John laid up, it was up to her and Billy to do the right thing, to try and prevent any bloodshed. They needed someone who commanded respect, a person who could stand up to both the farmers and the ranchers. Even as she debated the options in her mind, she knew the obvious conclusion. Luke Mallory was the best man for the job.

A warmth washed over her, like the bathing of a warm summer sun. She felt the heat spread upward to her cheeks, remembering how shamelessly she had succumbed to his kiss. Timony squirmed in the saddle, trying to access her own feelings.

She remembered the way Luke had cradled her in his arms after her accident with the wagon. The act had been one of caring and compassion, as tender as a father. She recalled sitting for hours in her room and holding her doll after that encounter. Then, after he had kissed her, she had gone to her room to reflect upon the event. Oddly, she no longer wanted to hold the doll. It had seemed an immature substitute for facing her true feelings.

Had the experience with Luke replaced her need for a mother? She immediately scoffed at the idea. She would always miss her mother. However, she no longer felt inclined to hug the toy and use it for comfort.

"All right, I can cope with that," she mumbled under her breath, "Luke isn't going to take the place of my not having a mother, but he sure enough has replaced my fondness for that doll!"

She turned her horse and started moving. Once she saw to John's comfort, she would go see Luke Mallory. Somehow, she had to convince him to stay in Broken Spoke. The hard part of that chore was she had to compete with his burning desire to become an agent for Wells Fargo. Luke had proven that he had a weakness for her, but would it be enough to overcome his lifelong desire to be someone important?

Chapter Thirteen

It had been an uneventful day, talking to the locals, acquiring mostly lame answers and no real suspicions. Luke ended up with one possible lead, but nothing concrete to tie anyone into the shooting of John Fairbourn. It seemed that no one had a bad word to say against the man.

Tired, and having spoken to everyone in town, Luke was ready to call it a night. He had removed his gun and hat, and was about to pull off his boots, when Cole stuck his head into the room. There was a sly look on his face, as if he had recently pulled off a major prank.

"You didn't say good night to Harlot," he said. "She's sulking around like she done lost her best friend."

"Speaking of that walking fur factory, how do you stand having cat hair on everything? I had so much hair sticking to my clothes that the mules didn't recognize me. About started a stampede when I got close to them!"

Cole chuckled. "Actually, there is someone here to

see you. I don't usually let prisoners have visitors, but you being a guest and all…"

Luke came to his feet at once and grabbed up his hat. "Who is it?"

"Best keep your gun handy" is all Cole said. Then he turned around and was gone.

Luke strapped on his gun, then walked through to the front office. Timony was standing inside the door. She displayed a trace of embarrassment, likely from coming to call on a man so late at night.

"Miss Fairbourn?"

"Do you wear your gun to bed?" she asked, looking at the weapon strapped to his hip.

"I was told I might need it," Luke replied, searching the room for Cole. He was not to be seen. *Off in a corner laughing himself sick,* Luke surmised.

"Can we speak privately?"

Luke continued across the room and opened the door for her. "Let's step outside. There's a cat in here who might take offense, if she thought you were going to rub up against me."

The crimson flush deepened within Timony's cheeks. "I don't think the cat has to worry about that."

Luke waited until Timony was outside, then closed the door. He led the way along the porch until they reached an alleyway. He paused to look both directions, then stepped into the passage. "This ought to be private enough."

"You are being awfully cautious."

"Secret of a long life is to not risk letting someone

shorten it for you. What brings you here at this time of night?"

Timony expelled a hesitant breath. "I thought you would be gone by now."

"Me too."

She lifted her head to peer at him. In the dark, Luke could not make out her expression, but he felt she was scrutinizing him, awaiting his explanation. When he let the words hang, she asked, "Why are you still here?"

"Maybe I couldn't bring myself to leave you," he said. "Is that good enough?"

"This is no time for jokes."

"The way I feel about you is no joke, Miss Fairbourn."

"Don't say that!"

Rather than get into a debate about his fondness for her, Luke turned to business. "All right, then, you do the talking. Why did you want to speak to me?"

"I came to ask ..." She hesitated. "I mean, there is something Billy thought you might be able to help us with."

"Me? Help with what?"

"When you reflect on it, it's partly your fault," she said, gaining strength to her voice. "You brought that horrible wire to Broken Spoke. You are the one responsible!"

"Responsible for what?" he asked. "I'm only a teamster for Wells Fargo. Delivering that load of wire was my job."

"But now it's starting a war!"

"I thought John was going to keep control of the situation."

"John won't be up and around for a month. Without him to ride herd on both the farmers and the ranchers, they have started fighting. Sally Cline was knocked into a barbed-wire fence by Sid Renikie, then Jimmy was beaten and their fence was torn down. On the other side, Big George's foreman was caught cutting wire at the Queen farm. He was worked over and sent home bound up in wire. We're about one step away from both sides shooting at each other."

"It makes a person wonder why John was the first target. Why take aim at the one guy who is trying to keep the peace?"

"John was admired by both the farmers and the ranchers. He's as well thought of as anyone in Broken Spoke."

"Okay," Luke said thoughtfully, "so we've determined that I'm Satan's spawn for bringing in wire, and that no one had sufficient cause to shoot your brother. That only leaves one more question: Why did you come to me?"

"You are neutral in the fight, and it will carry some weight if word gets around that you are going to be appointed to an agent position with Wells Fargo. As you told me, the title is one that nearly everyone will respect."

"There's a kick in the pants," he said. "You accuse me of having a fat head for wanting to be an agent, but it's okay to use the title when it suits your purpose."

It wasn't dark enough to hide her tight frown. "I'm trying to be logical here, Mr. Mallory. We need someone to mediate between the farmers and the ranchers. I came to ask you to be that someone."

He smiled. "Maybe you are only trying to keep me in Broken Spoke?"

"What? Why should I do that?"

"I think maybe you've got a hankering for me."

"Such a romantic term, *hankering!*"

Luke wished there was a little more light. He could see that Timony was making eye contact, but he was unable to read her expression.

"I could call it a yen."

"Sounds like a foreign kind of money."

"Soft spot then. Can we agree that you have a soft spot for me?"

"You're the one with the soft spot—right between your ears!"

"Okay, okay, we'll get back to the hankering. Now that we're in agreement that you do have some sort of feeling for me, what exactly do you want me to do?"

She appeared ready to argue the point, but got back to the original topic. "John said we should allow the farmers to put fences around their crops, so long as they don't cut off the free range and our cattle can get to the water holes. I detest the idea of wire, but if it could benefit both the ranchers and the farmers, it's worth at least trying. Better to give a new idea a try, rather than start a bloody war."

"And this job you have in mind for me?"

"Have Cole deputize you. You were once a deputy for Bill Hickok. No one is going to challenge you."

"I was a policeman, not a deputy."

"Mr. Mallory, this is serious."

"I'm serious as a busted tooth, ma'am. You're asking me to be a target. Tito Pacheco is a renowned gunman. He might challenge me to a fight. There are hotheads on both sides, the Renikie boys and the Queens. I could end up dead real sudden."

He could see that Timony was disappointed at his attitude. She lowered her head and her voice. "I can see I was wrong in coming here. I'm sorry to have troubled you, Mr. Mallory."

"It's no trouble." He decided the ruse had run its course. "I prefer to talk to you, rather than listen to Cole outline my duties."

"Duties?"

Pulling back his vest, he displayed the star on his chest. "I already pinned on a badge, Miss Fairbourn."

"You did what?" She was immediately fired up.

"I figured to ride out and talk with you tomorrow. If I'm going to do any good as a peacemaker, I'll need someone I can trust."

"Trust!" she stomped her foot and shook her small, doubled-up fist at him. "I ought to bust you one in the snoot! You let me grovel at your feet, when you had already taken on the job!"

"That was your idea of groveling?" He gave his head a negative shake. "You could stand to take some lessons. Cole has a cat who can show you how to really get down and grovel."

"You think this is funny, don't you?"

Luke took a step and made a grab for Timony. She was too quick for him, jumping back out of his reach.

"No you don't! I let you get too close the last time and lost a whole evening."

"I was of the opinion that you enjoyed it."

"Yes, well, I'm a proper young lady, and I'm not going to put myself in such a position a second time. If you wish to court me, you can ask John's permission."

Luke groaned. "If you recall, he's the one who tried to put both of my eyes on the same side of my head. Plus, he might also think I was the one who shot him. Not exactly my idea for making a good impression."

Timony backed into the street enough that she was standing in the light that came from Cole's office window. Her eyes shone with the luster of finely buffed sapphires. A spritelike smile danced on her sinuous lips.

"Perhaps I'll put in a good word for you, Mr. Mallory. At the moment, your competition to court me is Fess Renikie. He's more mature than you are, but you have the edge in appearance."

"You saying that you think I'm handsome?"

She shook her head. "I only gave you the edge, and not a very big one at that. I wouldn't want you thinking you were some kind of Don Juan."

"Of course not." Luke grinned. "He was a Spaniard."

"Good night"—she flashed a warm smile—"Mr. Mallory."

Luke watched her whirl about and mince swiftly up the street. He didn't care for the idea of her making the trip home in the dark, but she was a woman with a mind of her own. In any kind of relationship with her, a man would have to stay on his toes just to stay even.

Chapter Fourteen

Luke awoke when he felt soft jabs across his hips and stomach. He was roused from sleep to stare into the yellow-brown eyes of Cole's cat, Harlot. She plopped down her scruffy body right on his chest and began to purr.

"This ain't going to work," Luke said aloud. He began to rise, and Harlot dug in her claws to remain in her newly found bed. The cat refused to move, until he was so upright that she had to move or fall. She sprang onto his lap, gave him a look of disgust and swung about sticking her tail into his face. Then she waddled across the bed and jumped to the floor.

Luke dressed quickly and discovered that Cole was already up. He had a couple eggs frying in a skillet.

"You're actually cooking?" Luke asked, walking into the room.

"It's Sunday," he explained. "Even the Chinaman don't work on Sunday."

"I guess I lost track of the date."

"Cartwell has an idea to speak up for peace and

level heads at the Sunday meeting today. Ought to liven things up."

"He do the preaching?"

"There's a circuit parson who comes by once or twice a month. On the Sundays he don't show, Cartwell is in charge. He knows the words to most of the songs and plays the piano. On occasion, he delivers a fair sermon too."

"You think many of the farmers and ranchers will come in?"

"Not the Queen boys, and a few others don't usually show, but there's a pretty good turn out."

Luke sat down at the small table, noting that there were two plates and cups for coffee.

"Never got around to asking you last night, Mallory. Did you get any clues as to who might have shot John?"

"The lady who runs the laundry said her two Chinese workers spotted a horse tied up in the back alley. After the shots, the horse was gone."

"Could they identify the horse?"

"Chinese don't often ride a horse, Cole. Being such, they don't take the same notice of an animal as you or I might do. The one did say it had an odd coloring, mostly dark brown or black, with a blaze face and one ear that was white."

"That's something."

"I'll speak to Bunion and then take a look at the horses as they come into town today. Maybe we'll get lucky."

"Wouldn't be much to convict a man on, but it would give us a direction to work."

"I agree."

"By the way," Cole said, giving him a sidelong glance as he dished up the eggs, "what did Timony want last night?"

"She said there were a couple coyotes disturbing their young calves. I offered to give her your cat to get rid of them."

"Harlot couldn't whip a pair of coyotes."

Luke grinned. "No, but I figure they would sure enough strangle to death on a mouthful of her moth-eaten fur."

Cole uttered a grunt. "To hear you speak so poorly about her, I've a mind to not let her warm your feet at night."

"Could I get that in writing?"

"You've got a cold heart, Mallory. Eat your eggs before I decide to give them to the cat."

There was a good turnout for the meeting. Luke watched the different horses and wagons arrive, but he didn't see a horse to fit the description of the one in the alleyway. Bunion had been no help on that count. Of course, most of the ranchers had no reason to stable their horses with him. The only thing he was sure of was that the horse didn't belong to anyone in town.

Fess Renikie arrived in a buckboard, with Timony at his side. Luke watched as the man gave her a hand down, his teeth aching from the pressure of his clenched jaw. Fess was all smiles and was quick to take her hand as they entered the combination courthouse, saloon, and Sunday-meeting establishment together.

The Cline family entered a few minutes later, Dexter and his wife leading the way, with his boy and three girls following. Luke noticed the boy still had a yellowish coloring about one eye. Once inside, Leta sat next to her father, rather than being allowed to sit with Billy Fairbourn.

The two fractions were split down the middle, with nearly an equal number to either side of the room. The people who lived in Broken Spoke were scattered about, some supporting the farmers, some the ranchers, and a few who didn't show favoritism one way or the other. The tension in the room was thick enough that a stone statue would have buckled under the strain.

Luke was watching for trouble, but he could not prevent his attention from straying to Timony. More than once, she flicked a glance his way. The look in her eyes said more than any amount of words. He knew she was not sitting with Fess of her own accord. It caused a mixture of guilt and gratification that she was at Fess's side because of him. She had agreed to let Fess court her to squelch the possibility of raising a lynch mob. In essence, he owed that little lady his life.

Cartwell Devine took charge, stepping up behind the desk he had used as his courtroom pulpit. He began by offering up a prayer, then led the group in a song to praise the Lord. After the crowd had settled back down, he began his Sunday preaching. It had to do with the Golden Rule, but then he strayed toward the subject of the barbed wire.

"Friends and neighbors," he said, pleading with them, "even where fences are concerned, we can all live together in harmony. There is no need for fighting and violence."

"Tell that to the Queen boys!" Cully Deeks piped up bitterly. "I've got a dozen scars from that razor wire!"

"Don't you be throwing all the blame our way," Dexter said and snarled in return. "Your worthless pals hurt my Sally and beat on my son."

"You sodbusters started it!" another rancher cried out, leaping to his feet. "Who brought in that stinking devil's rope?"

"Who let their cattle stomp all over our fields?" Tom Kensington shouted back, rising to meet him.

"Hold on, people!" Cartwell tried to calm the crowd. "It's the Sabbath!"

But a tussle broke out between a young farmer and a cowboy. Luke might have been able to stop a one-on-one fistfight, but the confrontation escalated immediately. Before he had a chance to intervene, men and boys from both sides flew at one another. Even a couple of the women got into a pushing match and began to slap and pull one another's hair. Cole held up his hands and hobbled into the fray, but he was sent sprawling onto his face.

Cartwell shouted at the top of his lungs, but no one was listening to him. Punches were thrown, men were grappling about on the floor, chairs were scattered, and women and children screamed and fled from the building. From out of the mayhem, Cole crawled toward Luke on his hands and knees. He had lost his hat and there was a trickle of blood running from his nose.

"Fer the love of peaches, son!" he shouted. "Don't just sit there, Mallory!"

Luke saw that Fess had been considerate enough to get Timony out of the room. He gazed out into the brawling mass. Only a fool would wade into that kind of free-for-all.

"What would you have me do, Cole?"

"Stop them, Gall durn it! Stop them!"

Luke said something about the stupidity of such an order, but he spied a lamp and a stack of towels behind the bar. Quickly he kicked a clearing in the corner of the room, dumped the towels into a pile, and shook the oil over them. A second later, he put a match to the soaked material. Flames rose up instantly, and he kicked the heap enough to get it smoking good.

"Fire!" he yelled. "Get out! Fire!"

As smoke billowed upward and filled the room, the crowd ceased their fighting. Everyone scrambled out of the saloon. Within a few moments, men had quickly formed a bucket brigade to fight the fire. Luke was careful to keep it contained to a small area, so it took only a few trips with pails of water and the fire was out.

The interruption had accomplished its purpose. The farmers and ranchers had returned to their respective groups and were mostly heading home. The people from town stuck around long enough to make certain the fire was doused, then they too shuffled away.

"Well, I think it's safe to say that the Sunday meeting was less than a total success," Cartwell said to Luke, once the smoke had cleared out of the room.

"Sorry about your towels."

"They were less expensive than the furniture that was being busted up."

"Good thinking, starting the fire," Cole told Luke. "I was about trampled out there in the middle of the ruckus."

"What's your next move, Mallory?" Cartwell asked.

"I'll make the rounds of both the ranchers and the farmers. We need some form of understanding between them. If they won't agree to a reasonable solution, things are going to get a lot worse."

"I wish John was up and around," Cartwell said. "He was the only one who could talk to the ranchers."

"Reckon I'd best start with the farmers. By them stringing wire, they are the ones who have changed the status in the valley."

"Good luck, son," Cole said. "After the fiasco here today, I don't think anyone is going to want to listen to logic."

"I'll give them the rest of today to cool off. At first light tomorrow, I'll head out to speak to Cline. There has to be a way to stop the trouble, before we end up with a full-scale war."

* * *

Fess drove the buggy, consumed within his own little world of brooding quietude. Timony spent the journey staring out at the passing scenery, until he finally broke the silence.

"We need to draw up our plan of battle," he suggested. "The raids are going to start, now that war has been declared. Best have someone with your herd all the time."

"It doesn't have to come to that. You could keep the other ranchers in line."

"Why should I? The farmers have been asking for a fight!"

"There has to be a peaceful way to settle this, Fess."

"I think you should talk to John, Timmy. We have to get organized."

"I really dislike the name Timmy," she replied. "It makes me sound like a little boy."

"You never said nothing about it before."

"I didn't wish to be rude."

"You think I'm blind?" he asked abruptly. "I seen the way you kept looking over at that teamster. What's going on between you two?"

Timony glared at Fess. "I don't see any reason that I should have to answer a question like that. I agreed to let you take me to the Sunday meeting, that's all!"

"Don't be so bullheaded, Timmy," he said, purposely using the name she despised. "There's a fight coming, and you had best hitch your wagon to the prime team in the valley. You would be smart to side with me!"

"Side with you? I've got a family and ranch right here!"

"Billy and Token aren't going to be worth a pinch of salt in this-here fight. You've a couple hands that might hold their own in a scrap, but without John, you're a fruit tree ripe for picking."

"There's still a chance that there won't be a fight. Mr. Mallory pinned on a deputy badge. He is going to see about settling this feud without anyone being hurt."

Fess snorted his disdain. "The guy's a run-of-the-mill freighter, not no Texas Ranger."

"He was a deputy under Bill Hickok. I'm sure you've heard of him."

The dark expression that came into his face revealed that Fess was not happy about the news. "Who told you all this?"

"It doesn't matter."

"I think I know," he said, glowering at her, "you've got a flame burning for that teamster!"

Timony had taken about all she was going to. "I think you had better get me home, Mr. Renikie. I don't wish to talk to you anymore." With that, she put her back to him.

Fess turned his attention toward the team and road ahead, but she had glimpsed his face. It was a mask of hate; his eyes were a blistering red, and his mouth was twisted into an ugly sneer.

"You'll be sorry, Timmy." He hissed the words. "Believe me, the time will come that you'll want me at your side. You mark my words, when the fighting starts, you'll be begging to be with me."

She did not reply, once again staring out at the passing scenery. She had known beforehand that going with Fess was a mistake. He was pompous, full of mountain-size notions and words, with only an anthill-size brain to carry them out. She vowed not to give into his demands or trickery again.

Dexter Cline listened patiently while Luke explained the terms of a negotiated peace.

"What you say is true enough," he said, after Luke had finished, "but what about the damage done by them Renikie boys and Tito? We were of a mind to only save our fields. They done rode over here, hurt my youngest daughter, attacked my son, and tore out a whole section of fence."

"I'll be riding out to speak to all of the ranchers. John Fairbourn has already said that he will support you and the others in your efforts to protect your crops. However, the Queen family fenced off one of the major water holes. Then they beat up Big George's foreman for cutting their wire."

"Miller and his sons are troublemakers, same as the Renikie boys. We got hotheads on both sides."

Luke looked over to where two of the girls were doing laundry. The third was helping her mother to prepare bread for the oven. He had already seen the boy digging a hole to plant a post.

"I've heard that Leta and Billy have been seeing each other on a regular basis."

"They was, until the trouble started. Leta even let slip to Billy about the wire coming in." He lifted his shoulders in a slight shrug. "Guess you could say she was the one responsible for John whaling on you like he done."

"Hard to keep barbed wire a secret."

"I would have taken a strap to her for blabbing, but she's too old for that kind of discipline. I forbade her to see Billy for a month."

"I know you are the man to be a leader, Dexter. I'll look for you to lend a hand with the other farmers."

"I'll do as you ask and speak to the others, but the Queen family don't abide by no rules."

"Leave them to me."

He raised a skeptical eyebrow. "Them three will eat you alive."

"Maybe so, but they'll have a tough time swallowing."

"What about Tito and the Renikie boys?"

"I'll be riding up to see them too."

"You are walking into a den of lions with a handful of raw meat in either hand, Mallory. I'll give you credit for having grit in your craw, but courage alone ain't going to be enough. There's a fight coming."

"It's up to people like you and John Fairbourn to hold the line and prevent that."

"I'll do what I can, Mallory."

Luke took up the reins to his horse and mounted up. He raised a hand in farewell. Then he mentally recalled where the different ranches and farms were located. He wished there was time to ride out to the Fairbourn place, but he needed to talk to the trouble-makers on both sides first.

As Luke left the yard, Helen came out to stand next to Dexter. He felt her presence and finally turned to look at her.

"You're doing the right thing, dear," she said in a supportive tone of voice. "Mr. Mallory is right."

"For a little woman, you sure enough got big ears."

She smiled and took hold of his hand. "I have an interest in the welfare of our family too."

Dexter was amazed that a woman who worked so hard could still have such a light touch. He squeezed her delicate fingers gently within his callused hand.

"Guess I'd best saddle Pokey. I'll speak to the others and let Mallory talk to the Queen boys. It will add some meat to his warning, if they know they stand alone in a fight against the ranchers. It just might force them to listen to reason."

"I knew you were a smart man, when I married you."

He chuckled. "If I had been smart, I'd have gone into business with James and been working in a bank."

"This is our life, dear," Helen replied, "and I've never been sorry."

Dexter swallowed a rise of emotion. When he ordered the barbed wire, the crop had seemed all-important to him. In a flash of realization, he knew that he was holding the hand of what was most important to him in all the world. He had the responsibility to protect Helen and his children. It was an awesome burden.

"Throw something into a sack for me to eat on the trail, Helen. I probably won't get back home till late."

She leaned over and kissed him lightly on the cheek. "I'll have something ready by the time you get Pokey saddled."

Dexter looked after Mallory. He issued a silent prayer that the young man was capable of bringing order and sanity between the two factions. For himself, he had no fear about a fight, but a man had to think about the innocent who might be hurt.

"Good luck, sonny," he muttered. Then he was walking out to catch up Pokey.

Chapter Fifteen

Luke heard the shots and kicked his mount into a run. Bunion had given him a good horse. From the layout of the land given to him by Cole, he knew the shooting was coming from Tom Kensington's farm. He topped the rolling hill and saw three men. They were a few feet from their horses, each with a rifle, firing down at two men, who were using a wagon for cover.

Luke pulled his horse to stop and pulled his Winchester. Throwing it to his shoulder, he began pumping lead in the direction of the three attackers. Careful not to hit any of them, his arrival was enough to send them racing for their horses. Within a matter of seconds, they had beaten a path of retreat and were lost to the gently rolling hills.

Once certain the men were gone, Luke reined his horse down to Kensington's wagon. He was attending to the other man as Luke rode up. A glance told him the guy was not hurt seriously.

"You got here in the nick of time, teamster," Tom greeted him. "Those three had us pinned down."

"How's your friend?"

"I'm all right," the other man said. "Nicked me above the knee, but it's only a crease."

"They come over the hill a-shooting," Tom told him. "I expect this was another warning." He nodded at the wire in the wagon. "If you notice, we ain't started stringing wire yet."

"You say this was *another* warning?"

"Our milk cow was killed the other day. It had a note pinned to its tail."

"Let me guess, the note warned against stringing wire?"

"You got it."

"Could you make out any of those guys?"

"Sid Renikie was one," the wounded man said. "I recognized his dapple gray mare."

"Fess usually rides a black," Tom added. "I'd bet it was those two and one of their men."

The injured man was livid. "We'll sure enough pay them back, soon as I get this bandaged up."

"Durn right, Jeb," Tom agreed.

Luke tugged at his vest to show his badge. "I'm acting deputy sheriff for Broken Spoke, Mr. Kensington. I intend to put a stop to any fighting."

"And how would you be doing that?"

"All I'm asking is that you give me a couple days."

"They might have killed us both today."

"You said yourself, this was a warning. If they had been intending to kill you, they wouldn't have sat up on the rise and taken potshots at you two. The three of them could have come down and shot you close up."

"I reckon you have a point, teamster, but we can't sit back and take it. There comes a time to fight back."

"Like I said, give me a couple days to work out an agreement. Dexter will be over to see you in the next day or so. He's allowed that we try this my way first. If all else fails, there's always time to start killing one another."

"I'll abide by what Dexter has to say," Tom acquiesced, "but not for long. We're through taking it on the chin without fighting back."

Luke was satisfied that Tom was a man of his word. He said a short good-bye and headed off toward the Queen farm. Getting those men to follow suit would be the real test.

He swept the horizon, checking for any sign of the three ambushers. There was nothing moving within his sight, expect for a tendril of dust far back in the direction he had come. He paused to take a careful look, but he could see no one.

"Starting to see a rifleman behind every rock," he muttered. Then, with some irony, he decided that if he didn't put a stop to it, such a notion might well come to pass.

Timony was cut off by the three riders. She stopped her horse and waited until Fess, Sid, and Lynch, one of their hired hands, rode up to block her path. From the looks of their mounts, they had been doing some hard riding.

"Timmy, what are you doing way over here?" Fess asked.

She grit her teeth at his using the name *Timmy* again. "I've been over to visit with Big George and Von Gustin." She lifted her chin with defiance. "Both of them are going to allow the new deputy to propose a peaceful settlement."

"New deputy?" Sid asked.

"Yeah," Fess replied, "guess I forgot to mention it. The teamster pinned on a badge."

"Make a good target to shoot at," Lynch joked.

Fess put his attention on Timony. "I guess you're going to Fielding's ranch next?"

"Actually, Billy has gone to see him. If you recall, he has a dozen Basque workers shearing his sheep this week. He'd be in a fix if they were frightened off by a shooting war. I think he'll listen to what we have to say."

"Who made you the spokesman for us ranchers?" Fess jeered. "I don't recall any election."

"A woman's place is behind her man," Sid said pointedly. "Fess here is supposed to be your man."

"Maybe her man isn't one of the ranchers," Lynch said, narrowing his black eyes. "I think maybe it's the freight man."

"I don't have to sit here and be grilled by any of you," Timony shot back. "Billy and I have visited all of the other ranchers. Everyone is going to abide by the agreement. Are you, Fess?"

"What do you say, Sid?" Fess asked his brother.

"Think we ought to sit back and let some outsider come in and dictate terms to us?"

"I think it's time we took the bull by the horns, big brother. You were supposed to corral this little heifer, but now she's out stirring up the others, pitting them against us."

"Sid's right," Lynch agreed. "Her colors don't match the flag we're a-flying."

"I think you're running with that teamster's brand on your hip," Fess charged. "It's high time you decided where your true loyalties lie."

"I knew it would be a waste of time trying to talk to you," Timony answered back.

"There's a war brewing, Timmy. Ain't no one going to stop it."

"You won't last long, pitted against every farmer and rancher in the valley!"

"You'd best come over to our ranch, whilst we discuss it."

"Get out of my way!" she snapped, trying to ride through the three men.

Sid grabbed her horse's bridle to stop her. Timony used the reins to swat at him, but Fess had moved in on the opposite side. He caught hold of her arm and yanked her right off of her horse.

Timony fell to the ground, with Fess on top of her. She landed hard, knocking the wind out of her lungs. Before she could put up a struggle, Fess had pinned both of her arms.

"What do you think you're doing, Fess!" she demanded, panting. "Are you crazy?"

He glowered down at her, his eyes burning with the fire of derangement. He held her wrists so tightly, her fingers began to go numb. She had never seen such intense fury in his face before.

"What are we going to do with her?" Sid asked.

The question seemed to rouse Fess from his hateful trance. He relaxed his hold slightly. "Like I said, Timmy is going to come over to our place for a short visit. Once the fighting starts, she'll need a safe haven."

"You can't hold me against my will, Fess," Timony objected. "This is kidnapping!"

"Not much different than an elopement," he said thickly. Then, with a leer: "Who knows, it might end up that way before all is said and done."

"Billy will be looking for me."

Fess put on an innocent face. "The farmers must have grabbed you," he said. "We ain't seen you since the Sunday meeting."

"That's right!" Sid said with a laugh. "Don't know where you gone off to—maybe to run away with that teamster!"

The three men laughed, but Timony saw no humor in the dire situation. She knew Fess was sometimes wild, but this was beyond anything she had ever imagined. He was taking her captive!

Chapter Sixteen

Dory and Chad Queen were in the midst of stringing wire to repair a section of fence. Luke decided it was probably where Cully Deeks had been caught destroying the fence, as he was able to see a water hole a hundred yards or so away. He rode up to within a few feet of the two and climbed down.

"What do you want, teamster?" Dory asked, belligerently walking over to confront him.

"Yeah," Chad joined in. "We heard a rumor you was working with the ranchers."

"Got a piece of paper for you two," Luke bluffed, removing the voucher Dexter Cline had given him for the barbed wire delivery. "This here is a notice of my appointment as Deputy United States Marshal."

Dory frowned and stared hard at the paper.

"Is that what it says?" Chad asked.

Luke had guessed right that the Queen boys could not read. "The governor wants this settled without any bloodshed. That means you on this farm have to abide by the rules."

"What rules?"

Luke pointed at the fence. "This section of wire has to be removed. You have permission to fence in your crops, to protect them from cattle and sheep. However, none of the water holes are to be enclosed, and you are not to string wire that will prevent access to open range."

"You're full of road apples, Mallory!" Chad said and snarled. "You ain't telling us what we can do!"

Luke slipped his hand onto the butt of his gun. It was a casual stance, as if he was resting up from a hard ride. He measured the two boys, calculating their ability. They were lean and hard, but still young and inexperienced. Neither of them paid any attention to the fact the thong on his gun had been removed. He pointed with his left hand.

"I want you to pull up those posts and begin planting them in a line along the edge of your grain field."

"You want?" Chad laughed in contempt. "Here's all you'll get from us!"

Luke was ready. When Chad swung at him, he ducked the roundhouse swing and drew his gun. With an upward thrust, he caught Chad under the chin with the barrel. It sent him reeling over backward.

Dory attempted to jump him from the other side, but Luke came around with the pistol, slashing downward in an arch. As Dory got his hands on Luke's vest, the gun clubbed him alongside his temple. He staggered from the blow and dropped to his knees.

Luke stepped away from the two men, covering them both. "Attacking a United States Marshal is not a smart idea, boys. I reckon you're both under arrest."

Miller must have seen trouble brewing from the house. He came charging across the field on his horse. He had a rifle in one hand, but was careful not to point it in Luke's direction. Jerking his mount to a stop, he climbed down and took inventory of his sons. Both of them were back on their feet, each rubbing the lump on his head from being hit.

"What's the idea, Mallory?" he shouted. "I seen you pistol-whipping my boys!"

"Assault on an officer of the law, Miller."

"I didn't put no salt on him," Chad said tightly. "He was the one who salted us!"

"They attacked me, Miller, after I identified myself as a Deputy United States Marshal."

His eyes bugged. "I thought you was only Cole's deputy."

"I seen the paper," Dory told his father. "He's done got himself appointed as a U. S. Marshal."

"We sent off a wire to the governor," Luke said to decorate the story. "Cole didn't want to have to call in the Army."

"The Army?"

"There won't be any range war here in Broken Spoke, Miller. If it means locking your boys away for a couple years each, that's what we'll do."

He looked at his sons. "What are you talking about?"

"Assault on a peace officer will get them each a year or two busting rocks at the territorial prison."

"It's them what's doing the bleeding!" Miller objected. "You didn't even get hit!"

"Won't make any difference to a judge."

"Pa?" Dory was meek. "You ain't going to let him do this?"

"I don't want to go to no prison!" Chad also whined.

Miller held the rifle, but Luke still had his gun out. The farmer had no chance to get the drop on him, plus he didn't want the law down his neck for the rest of his life.

"What's the deal?" he asked Luke.

"I was explaining it to your sons, Miller. You pull up those posts and remove the fence that cuts off the water hole. The ranchers have agreed to let you put wire around your crops, so long as they have access to the water and can reach the grazing land beyond your farm."

"It'll take three times as many posts and wire."

"That's probably true."

Miller considered the option. "And what about my sons, Mallory?"

"You do as I ask and I'll forget that they jumped me." He put a stern look on his face. "But if you try and pull something, I'll be back with a posse. Your boys will end up in prison for a good long time."

"I expect we ain't going to fight no U. S. Marshal, Mallory."

"I'll be back by this way later," Luke told him. "I want to see those posts in a nice line along the edge of your planted fields."

"Yeah, yeah, we'll do as you say."

Luke studied the man for a few seconds. To turn

his back on such a man might be to get a bullet between the shoulders. However, he could see that Miller did seem to have a respect for the law. Either that, or he knew it would be a death sentence to shoot a marshal.

Mounting up, he turned his horse in the direction of Fielding's sheep ranch. It was time to make the rounds of the ranchers and confirm that they were going to abide by the same rules. Billy and Timony might have reached some of them, but he wanted his own personal assurance. Once he was convinced that the war had been averted, he could follow up on his appointment as an agent for Wells Fargo.

Timony was still aghast that Fess would dare take her to his ranch against her will. He did not tie her up or imprison her, obviously still intent upon winning her over.

"I want to go home, Fess," she said, after some time. "John will need me to look after him."

"Bunion and Token won't let him go hungry."

"You can't keep me here."

Fess appeared to be struggling with himself. "I only want to do what is best for you, for all of us, Timmy. Why can't you see that?"

"I'm a prisoner in your home, Fess. That's the only thing I can see."

He grabbed her by the shoulders, eyes glowing once more with an insane passion. "You're going to be mine, Timmy!" he exulted. "I'm going to make you my wife!"

"What a novel way you have for winning a girl's hand, Fess. Am I to be a captive at your house, until the wedding, or do you intend to hold me in chains the rest of my life?"

His fingers taloned into her arms until she winced from the pain. "You treat me like dirt under your feet!" he said snarling. "You can't see anyone except that freighter!"

"At least he treats me like a lady, Fess. You ought to try it sometime."

"I've tried everything!" he shouted. "You tease me, toy with me, even use me, whenever it suits your purpose. Remember your promise? I kept the men from hanging your teamster pal. I've done everything I can to please you, yet you still push me away."

"I'm sorry, Fess," she said, trying to remain calm, "but you can't force me to love you. I've never been dishonest with you about my feelings."

He shoved her away, hard enough that she banged into the wall. Fess was beyond reason, his teeth clenched in hate, eyes wild, nostrils flared with an uncontrollable fury.

"You will love me," he rasped vehemently. "Once the teamster is dead, when your ranch is in ashes, when the fighting and killing has spread all across Broken Spoke, you'll beg me to take you into my arms for love and protection!"

Timony stared at him in wide-eyed wonder. "You've lost your mind!"

"We'll see about that." He was yelling now.

"When the time comes, you'll be the one crawling to me!"

She did not dare speak, afraid that a single word might set him off. Fess had shown his desire for her ever since she matured into a young woman. He was beyond reason, possessed with an inner madness. She feared that he would never let her go.

Chapter Seventeen

Luke saw the rider on the trail ahead, coming toward him. As the man drew closer, he could see the horse was a stunning palomino, suited with a finely decorated saddle and a rhinestone-studded breast collar and bridle. The man wore an expensive leather vest that was decorated with conchos. His black sombrero-like headgear was embellished with an inch-wide silver hatband.

The man stopped crossways on the path, casually blocking the trail. A mirthless smile played along his lips while his eyes glowed with a curious expectation.

"The teamster man," he said easily, when Luke brought his own horse to a stop.

"You must be Tito Pacheco."

"That would be me. I thought you would have left town by this time."

"Cole thought he might need a hand, until this barbed-wire thing was settled."

"You are acting as a lawman?"

Luke stretched in the saddle and nonchalantly rested his hand on the butt of his gun, as if it was a comfortable position. "You might say that. I've been making the rounds of the farmers. Every last one of them has agreed to fence only their crops. Such being the case, I'm asking that the ranchers show a little understanding and allow them to protect their fields."

"Even the Queen family?"

Luke gave his head an affirmative nod. "Even them."

"Have you spoke to Mr. Fielding?"

"Not personally, but Billy and Timony Fairbourn have been making rounds to get the ranchers to be patient. I expect that one or the other has been to see him by this time."

Tito displayed a bit more of a smile. "Then this is your lucky day, Mallory."

"That right?"

Luke's eyes couldn't follow the movement. The blur of Tito's hand was swifter than the blinking of an eye. As if by some kind of magic, his gun was suddenly aimed right at Luke's chest!

"I could kill you with ease," he said in a matter-of-fact tone of voice. "Do you agree?"

Luke had to swallow against his heart, which had darted up into the base of his throat, as if seeking a hasty exit. He managed a shake of his head. "That's the quickest move I ever saw, Tito. You must have done a heap of practice over the years."

"Among other things."

"You speak very good English too," Luke said, changing the subject, making a futile effort to not look at the muzzle of his gun.

"I can read and speak French, English, and Spanish, Mallory."

"That puts you up on me by a pair. Where did you learn French?"

"When I was young and foolish, I joined the personal guard of Emperor Maximilian. He promised the Mexican people education and prosperity. For a hundred years, every previous ruler of Mexico had done the same, but I actually believed the French were serious." He lifted one shoulder in a careless shrug. "It didn't work out. The power was split between the church and the wealthy, so nothing was done for the people. When Maximilian was executed, I was branded an outlaw."

"So you left Mexico?"

"I took work as a payroll guard at a silver mine near the border, then worked as a sheriff in a town over in New Mexico." He showed amusement that Luke's mouth was agape at the news. "Lastly, my cousin contacted me about a job with Fielding. Here I am respected and have a good job."

"Does that job include knocking little girls into barbed-wire fences?"

The smile faded. "The Renikie boys haven't a brain between them. I warned them about doing something like that again."

"Warned them?"

"I told Sid that I would kill him," Tito said simply. "I think he believed me."

Luke swallowed again. This was a man he did not want to cross. "So what now?"

Wordlessly Tito holstered the weapon. "I suppose you should continue with what you were doing. If Fielding tells me to support you, I'll do that. If he says to kill you, I'll give you a chance to draw against me."

"With your speed, I wouldn't have a prayer."

The smile returned. "To the contrary, Mallory, you would have nothing but a prayer—a final one over your grave."

Luke began to go around Tito, but the man stopped him a second time.

"By the way, Mallory, did you know you're being followed?"

Craning his neck, Luke checked his back trail. "I've seen dust once or twice, even held up along the trail to watch, but never have gotten a look at them."

"I've seen the sun's reflection off of something at least twice. I think whoever it is, he's using field glasses, so he doesn't have to get too close."

"He hasn't come within rifle range, so I guess there isn't anything to worry about just yet."

"Before you head to the Renikie place, there's one more thing you ought to know, Mallory."

"And what's that?"

"Fess has Timony Fairbourn as his guest."

It took a moment for that to sink in. "His guest?"

"To call her anything else would be to call Fess a kidnapper. I don't think he intends her any harm."

"What happened?"

"I'm guessing he invited her to visit. When they rode into the ranch yard, Fess was leading her horse and she looked mighty unhappy."

"You weren't there when they grabbed her?"

"No, I was waiting for Fess at the ranch. His horse must have wandered off. I found him running wild in the hills, so I tossed a rope on him and delivered him home."

"You found his horse?"

"Recognized him from the markings. A half-Arabian mix, midnight black in color, except for a blaze face."

"And maybe one white ear?"

Tito blinked in surprise. "Yeah, one ear too." He frowned. "How do you know his horse?"

"I've heard mention of it before."

"Well, I'll be seeing you, Mallory. If you value your life, you won't turn your back on the Renikie boys."

"Thanks, I'll keep an eye on them."

Tito showed him a mirthless grin and nudged his horse with his heels. The animal responded at once, and he was quickly riding up toward the Fielding ranch.

Luke watched him for a bit, but his mind was not on the deadly gunman. Instead, he wondered about Fess Renikie's deranged thinking. Had he actually taken Timony to his ranch by force? If so, what did it mean? Was that the impulsive act of a total madman, or did he have something else in mind?

Luke wondered if he might have gotten word about the search for the horse in town. Knowing it was only a matter of time before someone remembered the coloring of his favorite mount, he might have seen the abduction of Timony as a way to lure Luke out to his ranch. Whatever his twisted notion, Luke was not going to let him keep Timony prisoner.

He took a few minutes to think out his next step. The lay of the land was to his advantage. The gentle, rolling hills gave way to an uneven bluff on one side and a fair-size ridge on the other. The trail to the Renikie place followed a beaten path between the two, allowing for him to drop below the sight of whoever was tracking him. Before he could plan a rescue, he first had to know who was behind him.

He put his horse into a gentle lope, as if he had made up his mind to ride down to the Renikie place. Once below the horizon, he kept watch for a place of concealment. It was only a short way before he saw a natural drainage ditch, where water ran after a heavy rain. It was large enough to hide his horse.

Luke picketed the animal up the ditch a few feet and took his Winchester from its scabbard. Then he waited for his shadow to appear.

Bunion came down the path a few minutes later, his eyes scanning the horizon and sweeping the ground in front of him. He was startled to come upon Luke, sitting patiently on the side of the trail, with a rifle across his lap.

"Mallory!" he said, jerking his horse to a halt. "You trying to stop my heart?"

"You've been following me for miles. Why the sneaking around?"

"Cole's idea," Bunion replied growling like an

awakened bear. "He said that you didn't want my help. I wasn't of a mind to make you feel put upon."

Luke chuckled. "Nonsense, Bunion. I'm glad you tagged along."

The old man squinted at him. "Yeah?"

"Fess Renikie has taken Timony to his ranch. According to Tito, she didn't go of her own free will."

"He kidnapped her?"

"Sounds like it."

"That Renikie pair are the worst vultures in the valley, but I never figured them for that sort of thing. What do you think?"

"It could be a ruse to draw me to them, or Fess might have lost what little sense he had."

"Wouldn't have been much of a loss. Never did trust either of them."

"You didn't tell me that Fess had a black horse with a blaze face."

"I don't recollect Fess ever leaving his horse at the livery. If he had, I'd have remembered." Then he realized what the news meant. "Black, with a blaze face," he repeated, "and maybe one white ear?"

"So Tito told me. Does that make any sense to you?"

"Fess always wanted to be the top dog in the pack. I reckon he saw that John was in the way. With him gone, he could take over as the head of the Ranchers Association."

"And, if I've heard right, John was also an obstacle to his courting Timony."

"So what's the plan?" Bunion asked. "Do we ride in and call them out?"

Luke surveyed the old man's Navy Colt, then looked at the single-shot buffalo gun strapped onto the side of his horse.

"Can you hit anything with that old rifle?"

"Could, until I commenced not being able to see things in the distance. I used field glasses to keep an eye on you."

Luke retrieved his horse and joined Bunion. "We don't have much of a case against Fess. Maybe you can slip in and come up to the Renikie place from behind. With luck, I'll get him to admit that he shot John from ambush."

"He ain't going to do that, unless he figures on killing you."

"That's why you have to come in from the back door, so to speak. Soon as he admits to the crime, you move in and get the drop on him."

"What about kidnapping Timony, sonny? If your gal will testify, we can put him behind bars for that."

"He might argue his way around that charge. With the possibility of a fighting war coming, he could claim he was protecting her."

Bunion rubbed the gray bush on his chin, his thick brows drawn together with his thinking. "I been to the Renikie place only one time, but I believe there is a ravine around to the back of their place. I might be able to come in with no one seeing me."

"How many men work for the Renikie brothers?"

"Three or four, but only one we need worry about.

His name's Lynch, and he's cut from the same bolt of cloth as them two. He'd back shoot you for a chew of tobacco."

"So, are you game?"

"Why not?" Bunion grunted. "I never expected to live forever nohow."

Chapter Eighteen

As he rode into the Renikie yard, Luke felt as if his body was encased in a shroud of pins and needles. His heart was hammering within his chest like the pounding of Indian war drums. It was insane to walk into a trap purposely, but he was going to free Timony, or die trying.

"That's far enough," a voice warned from off to one side of the house.

Luke turned carefully in that direction. Sid Renikie had a pistol pointed at him. "It seems that you are always pulling iron on me, Sid. You remember that the judge let me off the last time?"

"Too bad for you," he replied. "You might have lived longer in prison."

"I only came to speak to you and Fess about the farmers stringing their wire. Is Fess around?"

The door opened to the house. To Luke's surprise, Timony came out ahead of Fess. He stood next to her, a rifle in his hands and a dark scowl on his face. "You ain't welcome on our place, teamster."

"Howdy, Miss Fairbourn." He offered her a smile. "Never expected to run into you here."

She glanced back at his gun nervously. "Fess was nice enough to invite me over."

"What do you want, Mallory?" Fess demanded.

"You boys look ready for war, but there isn't going to be any fight. Everyone on both sides is in agreement about the wire. The farmers have agreed to use it only to protect their crops. No free range and no water holes are to be fenced off."

"You say," Fess said.

"This is my last stop. If you want to start a war, it'll be you boys against the rest of the valley. Rather long odds, even for a couple of tough men like you."

"Maybe you should leave, Mr. Mallory," Timony said quickly. "I'll stay here and discuss this with Fess."

Luke could tell that Timony was frightened. He had little chance against the two brothers while they had the drop on him. If Bunion managed to slip down unnoticed, the tables would be turned.

"I did have another question or two, Miss Fairbourn." He rested his hand on the butt of his gun, outwardly relaxed, while his stomach knotted with apprehension.

"Speak up and get moving." Sid was the one to answer. "What's your question?"

"Probably wondering where this guy was!" A new voice spoke up.

Luke's confidence took a dive. A man had Bunion

at gunpoint and was herding him into the yard from around the side of the house.

"I caught this fuzzy old wart a-creeping down the hill, tiptoeing like a cat slipping through a den of sleeping hounds."

"Good work, Lynch," Fess told him. Then he turned a sneer toward Luke. "Thought you'd pull a fast one on us, did you, Mallory?"

Luke's mind was racing, seeking any avenue that would gain him an advantage. With Bunion under Lynch's gun and both Fess and Sid covering him, he needed a diversion to have any chance against them. Stalling for time, he smiled.

"I wasn't sure you would let me say my piece, Renikie. If you aren't of a mind to listen, Bunion and I will head on back to town."

But Fess was not fooled. "You came here looking for trouble, freighter man. I don't think you're going anywhere."

Timony spun on Fess. "You promised! You said if I went along, you would let him leave!"

Fess was unmoved, his eyes never wavering from Luke. "You know more than you're saying, don't you, Mallory?"

"You mean about bringing Miss Fairbourn here against her will?"

The man bared his teeth. "Who told you that?"

Luke knew there was no getting around a fight. He remained outwardly relaxed, but every muscle in his-body tensed. It was impossible for him to take out all three men, but he could read the threat in Fess

Renikie's eyes. Fess was not going to allow him and Bunion to leave alive. Their only chance was to catch the men off-guard long enough to make a play.

"Actually, I came to arrest you for shooting John Fairbourn."

That surprised both Fess and Timony. Fess recovered quickly. "What are you talking about?"

"You rode your favorite horse that night, probably not even planning on an ambush. Then, when you spotted John in town, you decided to kill him and take over the Ranchers Association. You put your horse in the alley for a quick getaway, but the horse was seen by a couple of Chinese workers."

"You're talking crazy!" Fess shouted.

Timony was staring at him, unable to believe what she was hearing. Luke sought to gain whatever advantage he could from the situation.

"That's why you turned the horse loose out on the range. You hoped it would find its way to one of the nearby remudas and join up in a herd. It's likely that no one would have noticed an extra horse. Except Tito Pacheco found the horse first. He recognized it as being yours."

"You shot John?" Timony cried. "You tried to kill my brother?"

Luke saw her move as she attacked Fess, slapping and swinging at his face. He dropped his rifle to make a grab for her arms. At the same time, Sid's attention was drawn to their fight. Even Lynch had taken his eyes off of Luke. It was the only chance he was going to get.

Luke jerked his gun free of the holster. Sid saw him move. They both fired at nearly the same instant—

Something slammed into Luke, rocking him back in the saddle. He pulled the trigger a second time. The two slugs from his gun sent Sid staggering into the wall of the house.

Bunion tried to wrestle the gun from Lynch, but he was knocked to the ground. Timony ceased her assault at the sound of gunfire. Fess shoved her away and made a grab for his rifle.

Luke's horse danced about. He had gone numb on the right side and was unable to hold on to his gun. Lynch was next to fire at Luke. The bullet sang past his ear, but the horse jumped and unseated him. Luke landed on his right side and rolled over in the inch-deep dust. He vainly attempted to grasp his pistol with his good left arm.

The blast of two more quick shots caused Luke to freeze. He stopped in midmotion, with the gun still out of reach, expecting to feel the searing burn of the bullets that would end his life.

As the powdery cloud cleared before his eyes, he saw Fess and Lynch both lying on the ground!

"I think you should have asked for my help, Mallory." Tito Pacheco's voice reached his ears. "You sure enough made a sorry mess out of your rescue."

"Tito?" Luke gasped, overwhelmed with relief. "What are you doing here?"

Tito shrugged his shoulders as he holstered his still smoking gun. "Fielding said we ought to give this peace a chance. I figured you were in over your head, so I rode over to lend a hand."

"I'm mighty glad you did."

Timony was suddenly at Luke's side. She sat down and carefully lifted his head up onto her lap, trying to assess the damage.

"I guess our places are reversed," he said, looking up into her tear-glistening eyes. "I remember being the one to hold you like this, after your spill from the wagon."

"You silly fool," she said affectionately. "You ought to be dead right now. Whatever caused you to come here and try and take on the Renikie brothers?"

"They grabbed my girl," he returned curtly. "No one kidnaps my girl."

"I told you that you could come courting. I don't recall saying that I was your girl!"

Bunion was there now, peering over Timony's shoulder. "Don't look like you're hit too bad, sonny. I'll get my bag. I brung it along just in case things got ugly."

Luke turned his head so that he could see the Mexican gunman. "I reckon I owe you my life, Tito."

"John is a friend of mine," Tito said, shrugging off the thanks. "If I'd have known Fess shot him, I'd have come after him myself."

"I still owe you."

"If you want to do me a favor, put in a good word for me at Wells Fargo. I think this job is going to be right dull from now on."

Luke grinned. "There's a job as teamster open.

With only one good arm, I won't be able to drive the mule team back to Cheyenne."

Tito chuckled. "After we clean up around this place, I'll ride up and give notice to Fielding. I'll be ready to leave Broken Spoke when you are."

Luke gazed up at Timony again. "How about you? Will I see you again?"

She leaned down and kissed him gently. "You know where I live."